This wa***unted***
his slee *r so*
ago.

"Mitch Carver?" she said, dark eyes wide with shock.

"Darcy Connors," he replied. "Did I get the wrong office? Or are you just passing through?"

"What are you doing here?" she demanded. "I thought you said you'd never come back to Texas."

"I've said a lot of things I shouldn't have in my time," he admitted. For just a moment that unforgettable moonlit night flooded back. *Wow. Snap out of it,* he told himself sharply, remembering exactly why this woman was so dangerous to him.

"Well, here I am—in Terra Dulce," she said.

Here she was. Which meant they were going to be working in near proximity for the next year. He stopped for a moment, like a man checking out his body parts after a risky maneuver. Everything was still in one piece. Everything, that was, except his peace of mind.

It looked like he was going to have Darcy Connors back in his life, one way or another.

Dear Reader,

A tough guy from an old romance showing up on your doorstep, a past in Paris, a present in Texas and a pair of adorable twins in your life—sometimes, I wish I didn't just write these things. How fun to actually live them!

On second thought, the emotional highs and lows would surely wear me out pretty quickly. Much better to read about them than try to untangle them in your own life. That's exactly what makes fiction so much fun!

I hope you enjoy the ups and downs of the romance of Darcy Connors and Mitch Carver. He's the cousin of Grant Carver, whom you may have met when he reluctantly fell in love with Callie Stevens in *The Boss's Pregnancy Proposal*, out earlier this year. Love those Texas guys!

Happy reading!

Raye Morgan

RAYE MORGAN
The Boss's Double Trouble Twins

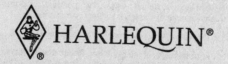

HARLEQUIN®

TORONTO • NEW YORK • LONDON
AMSTERDAM • PARIS • SYDNEY • HAMBURG
STOCKHOLM • ATHENS • TOKYO • MILAN • MADRID
PRAGUE • WARSAW • BUDAPEST • AUCKLAND

ISBN-13: 978-0-373-03988-3
ISBN-10:   0-373-03988-3

THE BOSS'S DOUBLE TROUBLE TWINS

First North American Publication 2007.

www.eHarlequin.com

Printed in U.S.A.

Raye Morgan is a fool for romance. And with four grown sons, love—or at least heavy-duty friendship—is constantly in the air. Two sons have recently married, which leaves two more to go, and lots of romantic turmoil to feed the idea machine. Raye has published more than seventy romances, and claims to have many more waiting in the wings. Though she's lived in Holland, Guam and Washington, D.C., she currently makes her home in Southern California, with her husband and the occasional son. When not writing, she can be found working feverishly on family genealogy and scrapbooking. So many pictures—so little time!

To the harried but happy mothers of twins everywhere.

CHAPTER ONE

MITCH CARVER hesitated as he came into the bright, shiny new chrome and glass office he'd been assigned. Everything in him was rebelling. How many times had he vowed he would never work here in his family's company? And yet, here he was.

He swore softly to himself, looking at the huge desk, the sleek computer, the neatly stacked books—the shackles of a businessman's life. And then he caught sight of himself in the reflection from the floor-to-ceiling window. He was wearing a suit, for God's sake. The hair that was usually long and untamed, the better to let him slip unnoticed into life on the wild side, had been trimmed short and neat. The beard and mustache were gone. It had been years since he'd looked so conventional. And he hated it.

"You win again, Dad," he muttered dryly. But only for one year. That was all he'd promised.

A sound turned his head. It was coming from what he assumed must be his new executive lounge. He stared at the closed door. He'd been told this entire floor was empty—a clean slate he was to fill with his own entrepreneurial genius, such as it was. Something—or someone—had been overlooked. There seemed to be humming going on.

A feminine voice sang out, low and bluesy.

Mitch cocked an eyebrow. This was interesting. The voice was incredibly sexy.

Then her voice trailed off as though she'd forgotten the words.

He bit back a grin. There was definitely a woman in his brand-new washroom. A stowaway. Maybe a squatter. And if she looked anything like she sounded… The hair on his arms was bristling—always a good sign.

Surely she hadn't been left here on purpose, just for him. But you never did know. This bore looking into and was certainly more interesting than any business he was going to be conducting today.

"Hello," he called out.

There was no answer, but suddenly a weird hush hung in the air.

"Who's there?" he tried again.

Nothing. He frowned. He couldn't leave it at that.

"I'm coming in," he warned, waited a moment for a response, then tried the door. It opened to his touch and there stood a young woman, dripping wet and naked except for a fat, fluffy towel, which was slipping precariously.

"Hey!" she cried, reaching quickly to stop the towel's impending dive toward the cold tile floor.

"You!" he said in turn, wondering for a fraction of a second if he was dreaming. This was a face, after all, that had haunted his sleep for months a year or so ago. A face—and a body—he couldn't forget, even while slogging his way through the Brazilian rain forest or trekking past the hidden villages that dotted the foothills of the Himalayas. He'd known her for how long? Less than forty-eight hours. And yet, out of all the women he'd ever met, she'd stuck in his thoughts like…like the refrain of a low, bluesy song you couldn't get out of your mind.

Yeah, he told himself cynically. A guilty conscience will do that to you.

Guilty for treating a woman such as this like a one-night-stand. Guilty for seducing a woman whose relationship to an old friend had never been made exactly clear. Guilty for letting a strong attraction take over and push away all concerns about anything but his own raging desire. He could try to blame it on the exotic intoxication of a Paris night, but he knew very well it had been his own fault. She'd bewitched him, but he'd asked for it.

"Mitch Carver?" she said, dark eyes wide with shock.

He grimaced. The feeling was mutual. No one liked to face a reminder of his own weakness.

"Darcy Connors," he recalled, noting her confirmation as she nodded, looking numb. "Did I get the wrong office?" he asked her quizzically. "Or are you just passing through?"

She was still staring at him as though she were seeing a ghost.

He shrugged. "Never mind. I'm always happy to share with an old…uh…friend," he said, silently cursing himself for hesitating before the word. "Carry on. I'll just go and…"

"What are you doing here?" she demanded, clutching the towel up to her chin. "I thought you said you'd never come back to Texas."

He wasn't any happier to see her than she was to see him, but he was beginning to feel she was overdoing it a bit. The tragic look she was giving him was hardly fair. After all, he wasn't an ax murderer or anything like that.

"I've said a lot of things I shouldn't have in my time," he admitted. "Things change. Sometimes you've got to eat a little crow. See this?" He gestured toward his mouth. "Covered with feathers at the moment. That was one tough bird."

She frowned as though she was still too surprised at seeing him to get his little joke. He took in all of her, the dripping hair, the shimmering drops on her thick eyelashes, the creamy skin and those long, lovely, silky legs he remembered from that moonlit night.

That unforgettable moonlit night. For just a moment it flooded back, the soft air, the sound of water parting as the Bateau Mouche moved along the Seine, a distant jazz singer, notes from an accordion, lights making patterns against a set of statues, trees, wrought-iron balconies. She'd shivered slightly and he'd put his arm around her shoulders, pulling her close to keep off the chill. She'd curled up against him and whispered something and he'd laughed, catching her scent and turning....

Wow. Snap out of it, he told himself sharply, remembering exactly why this woman was so dangerous to him. For some reason she'd appealed to his senses in a basic, primal way he couldn't ignore. And looking at her now, he knew nothing had changed. Everything about her seemed to tug at his libido.

And that just didn't make any sense. She wasn't his type at all. She had "happily ever after" written all over her. And he was a "here today, gone tomorrow" type of guy. Oil and water. They didn't mix well and it was dangerous to try. At least that was the way it was in his world.

"So you're not in France anymore," he noted.

She stared at him so intensely, he almost took a step backward, and at the same time, he realized there was one thing that *had* changed. She'd fallen for him that night just as hard as he'd tumbled for her. He'd seen it in her eyes, felt it in every move she made. But that was all gone now. Her gaze was wary and speculative. Her body language was defensive. She looked like a woman who expected to be under attack. And she definitely wished he hadn't shown up on her doorstep.

That triggered his curiosity. He knew why he wanted to stay away from her. But why did she want to stay away from him? Was she angry that he hadn't tried to contact her in the last two years? Or did it have something to do with that same guilt he was feeling?

"No, I'm not in France anymore," she admitted. "I transferred to Atlanta first, but they needed me here, so I packed up again and moved to the San Antonio area. And here I am, in Terra Dulce."

Here she was. Which meant they were going to be working in near proximity for the next year. He nodded, not really sure why that gave him such a feeling of foreboding. After all, when you came right down to it, they hardly knew each other. Just because they'd shared that one night in Paris didn't mean they had to be buddies. They didn't have to see each other socially just because they had both landed back in the same town. They would probably just greet each other in the halls now and then and leave it at that. He wasn't going to be here all that long, anyway. Keep it casual. That was the ticket.

"I heard about what happened to Jimmy," he said softly, mentioning the friend whose Paris apartment was the place he and Darcy had met. Jimmy had been killed in a race car incident just days after Mitch had left France for Brazil. "Sorry I didn't hear in time to make the funeral."

She looked nonplussed for a moment, then nodded.

He could have said more. He could have explained that he was in a South American jail about the time Jimmy was being eulogized, not sure if he was going to make it out alive himself. Of course, he obviously had been released. The odd time in various jails was just one of the minor drawbacks of his chosen line of work. But that seemed a bit much to lay on her at the moment.

Jimmy had been their tie, and at the same time, what might now stand between them. Mitch and Jimmy had been childhood friends. They'd lost touch after high school, but he'd heard that Jimmy was working in Paris, and when he was passing through, he'd looked him up. He'd found his old friend changed and a bit distant, but he'd also found Darcy. She was living with Jimmy but it was never clear to him just what their relationship was, and he had to admit, he hadn't really wanted to know. She had seemed eager to get out of the tiny, cramped apartment so the two of them had left Jimmy behind and taken in the sights and sounds of the French city. Very quickly it had been as though Jimmy didn't exist. For the next day and a half, they had been so wrapped up in each other, nothing else seemed to matter.

"He was a great guy," he said gruffly.

She winced, then nodded again, biting her lip. "Yes. It was a shame." But after a moment, she was issuing a significant look his way. "Do you mind?" she said, nodding toward her towel.

"Oh. Sure. Sorry." He started to close the door, then stopped. "Wait a minute. You haven't told me what you're doing here. I thought this was my new office."

She blinked at him, searching for words. "I… uh…" She shrugged helplessly. "I was the victim of an industrial accident. One of our financial department geniuses dumped his café latte on me."

He stared at her. "From head to toe?" he asked, noting her wet hair.

She nodded. "He was on the second floor catwalk and I was down in the lobby…."

"Okay. I get the picture." He couldn't resist a quick grin. "He must have been really mad at you."

She opened her mouth, obviously to protest his characterization of the incident, but he held up a hand. "Never mind. I'll leave you to your grooming tasks. Nice to see you again, Darcy."

She'd been turning away but her head snapped back around at that, as though she thought she might have caught a joking reference to her too-revealing appearance and she glared as he quickly closed the door.

Once outside, he stopped for a moment, like a man checking out his body parts after a risky maneuver. Everything was still in one piece. Everything, that was, except his peace of mind. It looked like he was going to have Darcy Connors back in his life, one way or another. And that was something he hadn't counted on. When he'd agreed to come back and work in his family's company he had assumed Darcy was still in Paris. It hadn't occurred to him that she might be working at the home office.

He took a deep breath and told himself things would be different. He wasn't passing through on his way to danger and adventure this time. He had other things on his mind and a better perspective. He wasn't going to let a provocative woman tangle up his emotions. He would keep his libido in check.

But damn! It wasn't going to be easy. There was something about that woman that appealed to him in ways he didn't understand. And that low, sexy voice just knocked him out. *It* appealed to him in ways he understood too well.

Steady, he warned himself.

Straightening his tie, he started for the elevator. He didn't want to be standing here waiting when she emerged.

Darcy was in shock. Mitch Carver was back. The man who had been unreachable, unfindable and unfathomable for the last two years was suddenly back and very much available, and that meant she was finally going to have to do what she'd been unable to do all this time—tell him about the twins.

Of course she had to tell him. But… A feeling very like panic fluttered in her chest. Yes, she was going to tell him, but not right now. She wasn't ready. She hadn't prepared. She'd pretty much accepted that it might never be possible to tell him. And now, suddenly, it was. So how was she going to do this?

She groaned, her shoulders slumping. If only she'd had some warning. Lately it seemed everything came at her so fast, she was never ready. And that meant she always seemed to do the wrong thing. Like this morning. Knowing the office was empty and unused, she'd been sure she would have time for a quick shower before anyone even noticed her missing from her desk on the second floor. And what happened? Mitch Carver showed up to catch her at it. Of all people! She'd never dreamed that could happen.

When she'd heard a Mr. Carver was coming in to take over Property Acquisitions, she'd assumed it was Craig Carver, Mitch's cousin, who she'd heard was transferring from the Dallas branch of the family firm. She'd never met Craig. Unfortunately she couldn't say the same about Mitch.

Closing her eyes, she swayed in silent agony. How was she going to do this? How was she going to tell this man she barely knew that he was the father of her two children? That what had seemed like a romantic interlude, a chance encounter, a fleeting intimacy, had turned into a lifetime commitment? One mistake, one night of letting down her legendary guard, a one-time retreat from a lifetime of caution, and she was destined to pay the price forever. And so was he.

Not that her babies weren't worth it. She couldn't even think about them without smiling.

They were her joy, her life. But their father was her dilemma and her complication. And now she had to tell this man who had made no secret of his determination never to settle down, never to live a conventional life, that he had a pair of anchors, whether he liked it or not.

She knew he wouldn't be happy about it. Would he hate her? Hate them? It was clear he wouldn't want to let anything as mundane as children get in the way of his work. She wasn't real clear on just what he did out there in the world. She had the impression he went where people paid for his services, but she was also pretty sure he spent more time using his brain than his brawn. Nevertheless, there was plenty of danger involved, and she knew from what he'd told her that the excitement was intoxicating to him. He loved it. So what was he doing here?

A speedy wipe-down with the towel and then she was slipping into the fresh clothes her friend Marty had supplied: a jersey top and a cute denim skirt. Both were a little large for her slim figure, but they would do.

She rolled the soggy dress she'd worn to work that day in the towel, fluffed her shoulder-length blond hair under the wall hair dryer for a few minutes and peeked out into the office to see who was there.

No one. Super. In just moments she was back on her own floor, her own desk in her sights, when someone called from behind.

"Hey, Darcy!"

It was Kevin, he of the errant café latte. She kept walking, but he caught up with her.

"Hey, I really, really am sorry."

He looked sorry. He was young and bright and he seemed to have something of a crush on her, but he certainly did look sorry.

"Forget it," she said shortly, reaching out to pick up the papers filling her in-box.

"Really Darcy, it was an accident. I just leaned over the rail to look at you and the cup slipped and…"

"Sure, Kevin. I understand. Don't think another thing about it." She began riffling through the papers, though she didn't see a thing. She was wondering where Mitch was—mainly so that she could avoid him. She needed time to think.

"I'd love to make it up to you, Darcy," Kevin was saying, looking puppy-dog hopeful. "I thought maybe I could take you out to…"

Kevin's suggested destination was to remain forever unknown. Before he got the name out, the elevator doors across from her office opened and Bill Monroe, her amiable boss, stepped into their conversation.

"My office, Darcy," he said, cocking a stern fore-finger her way. "Right now."

"But…" She glanced at the clock on the wall over the elevator. "I really don't have time this morning. I'm running a little late and I've got people waiting for some research I've been doing and—"

"Forget that," Bill said flatly. "I need to talk to you right away."

There was a grim look on his normally jovial face as he headed for his office. Kevin shrugged dejectedly and disappeared down the stairs. Darcy sighed, stowed her things away and looked up to find Mitch coming toward her.

"Oh, hi," she said awkwardly. It gave her quite a start to have him casually turning up where she wasn't used to seeing him. It also gave her an opportunity to really look at him, and for a moment, that was what she did.

He looked so different, it was a wonder she'd recognized him right away. She flashed back to that weekend in Paris and what he'd looked like then. She'd been sharing a small place with Jimmy ever since she'd arrived in Paris. Apartments were impossible to find in the area near where they both worked at the same company. Their mothers had been best friends, so they'd known each other forever, and it had seemed only natural to share a place.

When she'd heard that Mitch was dropping by, she'd had a few seconds of excitement before she'd reminded herself that he wasn't coming to see her. He probably didn't even remember who she was. So when the doorbell had rung, she'd gone to let him in, not expecting much but pleased to be seeing someone from home. Opening the door, she'd found him standing there and her world had fallen out of the sky.

He'd been completely wild, totally exotic, like a fictional hero. His hair was a long, thick tangle framing his outrageously handsome face. His body had been spectacularly displayed in a tight, clinging shirt and torn jeans that molded to his muscular legs like something that had grown to cover him. He was reeking with attitude and looked like a young freedom fighter, a rebel, a revolutionary, ducking in out of the street to evade a pursuer. Even now, the memory of how provocatively fine he'd looked took her breath away.

She'd fallen for him like a ton of bricks, right there in the doorway to Jimmy's tiny flat. Not that it should have been surprising. After all, even though she hadn't seen him for years, she'd had a crush on him since she'd been a child. Of course, he'd never noticed her in those days.

Only, this time he did.

"Hey," he'd said, looking deep into her eyes.

"Hey yourself," she'd said back, looking dreamily into his.

"What's your name?" he'd asked, proving her theory.

"Darcy," she'd responded, just as glad he didn't remember the awkward girl who'd mooned after him in the old days.

"I'm Mitch."

"I know."

He'd smiled and she'd swooned toward him.

"Want to run away with me?" he asked her softly, leaning even closer.

She'd nodded without hesitation, knowing it was just banter, but answering in all sincerity. "Yes," she whispered.

His gaze had seemed to devour her hungrily and for one long moment, she'd lost herself in his blue eyes.

"Hey, Mitch," Jimmy had called out from the kitchen. "You finally got here."

And she'd pulled back, thinking the moment was over, that the relationship between the two men would be the focus of the rest of the day. But she'd been wrong. The magic that had sparked between them didn't fade. As soon as they got the chance, they'd gone out into the city together, and things had gone from pure delight to rapture.

At first she'd looked on that exciting weekend as a mistake, but one that was just too delicious to really regret—a romantic episode she would treasure forever. It seemed the kind of thing you read about in books or saw in movies. He'd come into her life at just the moment she had felt most lost and lonely and reminded her of what joy in living could be like—and then he'd gone.

And then she'd realized she was pregnant.

She watched as he approached her now, looking so clean-cut and handsome—not a rebel at all. But she knew that exciting body still lay under the suit coat and hints of that crazy untamed spirit still lurked in his eyes if you looked hard enough. The packaging had changed, but he was still the same guy.

Was she still the same girl? Not on your life.

CHAPTER TWO

"WHAT are you doing on this floor?" Darcy asked for lack of anything better to say.

Mitch shrugged. "I got a message from Bill Monroe." He noted the startled look on her face in reaction to that news. "You, too?"

She nodded. A feeling of dread was beginning to build inside her. If this was what she thought it might be...

He inclined his head. "Lead on, McDuff," he muttered.

She bit her lip and led the way into her boss's office. Bill rose and shook hands with Mitch, murmuring a greeting. Still standing, he got to the point.

"Darcy, I hate to lose you. But you've been assigned to the new department Mitch will be heading."

She blanched, though by now she'd been expecting this very thing. "What?" She shook her head. Surely this wasn't written in stone yet. "No." She turned to Mitch appealingly. "No!" Surely he would do something to stop this.

And he looked as though he wanted to. "Interesting," he said. "But there's been some mistake. You see, I won't need an assistant. I've already got a secretary picked out and—"

"Darcy isn't a secretary. She's a property analyst. And her area of expertise resides smack dab in the center of your new project." Bill dropped an armful of folders on the desk as though that settled the matter. "You can take these with you."

Darcy's heart sank. That meant Mitch was taking over the Bermuda Woods development. She'd been working on that one for months. There was no way she was going to get out of this, was there? She stared into Mitch's eyes and he stared right back into hers. She'd forgotten how gorgeous those eyes were, deep blue and dangerous as the sky on a stormy day. Those eyes were the first thing that had intrigued her when she'd met him in Paris. She winced.

Don't think about Paris, she told herself sharply. Not now.

"You know, I really can't do this," she said, looking at her boss brightly, giving it one last try. "I've got a desk full of work. Mr. Grayson is waiting for my report on the Clemson release."

The older man glowered at her. "Sorry, Darcy," he said stiffly. "You've been assigned to Mr. Carver.

You can take it up with the board, but as far as HR is concerned, you're working up there now."

She swallowed hard and tried to smile. The man was droning on, giving Mitch some last-minute instructions on paperwork, but she wasn't listening. This was disastrous. She couldn't work for Mitch. She could barely look at him. Once he'd found out about the twins…

"They want these forms to be filled out before you leave this evening," Bill was saying to Mitch. He sent a regretful look Darcy's way. "I hate to see you go," he told her, "but my loss is Mitch Carver's gain." He smiled at the younger man. "Her expertise is going to be invaluable to you. You'll see that soon enough."

Nice words, but she hardly heard them. She took up the folders and carried them back to her own desk, the one she was going to spend the day clearing out. Mitch came behind her.

"Want me to carry some of those on up for you?" he asked.

When she flashed him a look, he added, "Look, Darcy, I'm not any crazier about this than you are."

She turned on him, thinking if that was really the case, he could have tried a little harder. "You ought to have some pull, being the boss's son and all. Can't you do something about this?"

He grimaced, raking fingers through his thick hair distractedly. "I'm pretty much in the position of the

returning prodigal right now. I don't have too many
favors owed me. But I'll see what I can do."

"Good." That seemed to be all she wrote as far as
rays of hope were concerned. She didn't think
holding her breath until she turned blue would be ef-
fective at this point. "You've got to do something."

"Do I?" Turning back toward her, he cocked an
eyebrow.

"Yes. Of course. You know we can't work together."

"Can't we?"

He looked genuinely puzzled and she realized he
had no clue why she might feel that way. Not yet,
anyway. Once he knew about the twins, he would
understand. She was going to tell him…just as soon
as she figured out how.

But that was just the problem. She had no idea
what his reaction would be. She knew he didn't want
a family. He'd been very clear on the point that night
when it had seemed they were opening their hearts
to each other. So he wasn't likely to take this as good
news. She'd assumed he would resent her dropping
this bombshell in his lap—maybe even try to wriggle
out of facing it. But he didn't know about them yet,
so why was he acting as though he wanted to keep
distance between them as much as she did? She could
think of only one possible reason—he was afraid she
might want to resume their affair and he didn't want
any part of that.

Just the thought of that sparked a flash of anger,

but she pushed it back. After all, wasn't that exactly what she was feeling as well?

"I'll do what I can," he was saying, turning to go. "I'll let you know."

She nodded and watched as he strode toward the elevator.

"Who's the hottie?" asked a voice at her elbow.

She started, then grinned feebly at Cindy, her officemate who had come up to stand beside her.

"Looks like he might be my new boss," she said ruefully.

Cindy laughed, shaking back her thick, ebony hair. "Oh the agony of it all," she said, amusement dancing in her green eyes. "Listen, I'm willing to take your place if it will make you feel better."

"I'll keep that in mind," Darcy said, wishing that sort of trade was actually possible. But once she'd heard what Mitch's assigned area would be, she knew she was on shaky ground for a transfer. This was her project. Getting *him* transferred would be more logical. And that hardly seemed likely.

Still, there had to be some way.

Mitch should have felt right at home in the sleek offices of ACW Properties. His grandfather had started the company sixty years ago. His father had been CEO of the San Antonio branch ever since he could remember. He'd played in these halls as a child, had part-time jobs here in high school, did a summer internship. And in those days, it had all seemed natural to him.

But his relationship with his father had been destroyed shortly after his freshman year at college. In reaction, he'd rejected every part of the life his family had expected him to follow. Coming back now had been a bitter pill to swallow. It had taken emotional blackmail to make him do it.

Now he was being escorted through the building by Tanya Gayle, the long and lanky director of Human Resources. She'd offered to give him a tour of all the new facilities and from her sideways glances, he had a feeling she was offering a lot more than that. Luckily, once he'd realized he wasn't going to get out of it, he'd had the presence of mind to bring along Paula Pinter, his new secretary and the woman who had baby-sat for him here in the office as a child. There was nothing like the addition of a sweet, gray-haired older woman to tamp down the fires of office romance.

Tanya escorted him into the workout room as though she'd been personally responsible for it herself, explaining as she went how it was company policy that each employee take an extra fifteen minutes at lunch to get in some exercise.

"Really. Who made that decision?"

"Your father, I imagine."

"No kidding."

Mitch raised an eyebrow. That seemed a bit ironic,

considering the way his father used to spend his lunch hours in the old days.

The Carvers had always been community leaders. To the outside world, they looked like an ideal family. But the public face had been in many ways a false one. Mitch and his brother Dylan spent part of their youth covering up the truth about their father's drinking and the ugly fights that sometimes tore apart their homelife.

Pushing away bad memories, he glanced around the room, noting a full complement of employees in colorful workout uniforms. And then his eye was caught by Darcy on a treadmill. She had on earphones and was working hard, looking determined. He watched her for a moment. Paula noticed where his gaze was directed.

"That's Darcy Connors," she said helpfully. "She's down here every day, a real role model to us all."

"Yes, she's worked hard to get back that trim and girlish figure," Tanya chimed in. "And she's done a great job. We're all jealous."

Mitch frowned. Get back her girlish figure? Where'd it gone? It had certainly been present when he'd known her before. He turned to ask Tanya what she meant, but Paula had pulled out a bright jersey tank top in the company colors with his name on it.

"Surprise!" they said in unison.

He swallowed his question and tried to look pleased.

"Put it on," Paula urged.

"Right now? Right here?"

"Why not? Come on. We'll see if it fits."

He shrugged. Why not, indeed? He was here for the year and he might as well make the best of it. Fitting in with the crowd was part of that, he supposed. So instead of getting his exercise racing after bad guys in the jungle, he was going to get on machines, was he? Oh well. Yanking off his tie, he began working on the buttons of his shirt.

Darcy had developed the habit of spending most of her lunch hour on the treadmill. Not only did she get a good workout, but it also gave her the time and space to set her mind free and think things through. And today she had a lot to think about.

All the other machines were filled with other employees. She paid no attention to them, but when Mitch arrived in the room, somehow she sensed it. Biting her lip, she tried to stay focused and ignore him. But finally she had to turn her head, just in time to see him begin to pull off his crisp white shirt. She held her breath, and when she realized what she was doing, she closed her eyes for a moment, cursing softly.

When she opened them again, she saw that beautiful body and steeled herself. And then she saw something else. There across his chest was a jagged line of scarring that she knew hadn't been there when she'd known him. It looked fiery and painful and she gasped so loud, heads turned all up and down the room. He looked up and her gaze locked with his, but only for seconds.

She stumbled on the treadmill, losing her pace and almost losing her balance, her heart beating wildly. That beautiful body and that ugly scar. His skin had been smooth and flawless when she'd last seen it, touched it. What on earth had happened to him?

She drew a deep breath, reminding herself she wasn't going to let emotions tangle up her life again. Whatever had happened to him was none of her business. She had two babies to raise and protect and that was enough for her to deal with.

Turning up the mileage on the treadmill, she worked harder, hoping to blot out his presence on the other side of the room. But she was beginning to wonder if she was ever going to be free of him again. And suddenly her mind was full of what it had been like two years before, right after Mitch had left for South America.

She'd been walking on air. Of course he'd told her he wasn't in the market for a lasting relationship, and she'd accepted that at the time. But something deep inside had whispered lies of wishful thinking to her. Those two days had been magic. She'd never known a man like Mitch, never felt the crazy excitement, the overwhelming affection, the deep and undeniable need she'd felt with him. They had been so good together. She knew he felt the same way. She knew he was just as reluctant to leave her as she had been to let him go. She'd been so sure he would contact her again, despite everything he'd said. How could two people fall madly into love for a weekend and then walk away without a backward glance? It just didn't seem possible.

One week went by. Then another. She was still so sure that she would hear from him soon. With Jimmy totally wrapped up in his racing, spending every free moment at the track, and things at work more difficult than she'd ever expected, she felt very much alone. And then came the horrible afternoon when Jimmy's Formula One car crashed during a practice run. He was rushed to the hospital and died later that night. Darcy had been the one to call his mother with the news—the one to accompany his body back to Texas, the one who supported his mother at the funeral. For days that was all she could think about.

And then she realized she was pregnant.

By then Mitch had seemed very far away. And when she couldn't find him or get in touch with him, she began to resent him—as though he'd done this to her and then run out on his responsibilities. Again, it was like something out of a book or a movie, only now it had turned from romance to dark drama. A character study in male dependability.

She'd had her babies. She'd gone through it all alone. It wasn't easy, but she was managing. And suddenly, he'd turned up again.

It was all wrong. Things weren't happening in

the right order. If only she'd been able to get hold of him right when she realized the babies were on the way. She knew he had no interest in being a father. He'd told her as much that night in Paris—and by the time she knew she was pregnant, she was ready to believe what he'd said was the last word after all. She wouldn't have asked all that much of him. But at least he would have been moral support. She wouldn't have had to make all the decisions on her own. There would have been someone to share things with, even if just in letters or phone calls.

Okay, she was starting to sound whiny now, even to herself. Enough. This was a situation, but she could handle it. She'd toughened a lot over the last two years. She'd handled everything up to now pretty well, hadn't she? And she could do this, too.

Turning off the machine, she grabbed a towel, wiped her face, then threw it around her shoulders, turning to step off. And there was Mitch, waiting for her.

Her eyes widened, but she didn't stop.

"Are you stalking me?" she asked, brushing past him and trying to ignore the lovely bulging muscles his company tank top revealed.

"I'd only be doing that if you were avoiding me," he pointed out. "Are you?"

Turning back, she looked at him. Her first thought was that he had some nerve accusing *her* of being ellusive. He was the original Houdini in her life. But as her gaze met his, she felt her resentment melting. It was those huge blue eyes with those gorgeous dark lashes. She was a sucker for that look—always had been.

"No, of course not," she said. And silently, she raged at herself. *"Wimp!"*

"Good. Because I think we need to talk. Why don't you meet me in my office in half an hour?"

She nodded. This was it. Her heart was pounding. "Okay," she said, then turned and marched toward the women's locker room.

He was right. They did need to talk, about so many things. The question was, should she tell him now? *Could* she tell him now?

"We'll play it by ear," she told herself reassuringly as she slipped into her work clothes. But that was no good. She knew she was just giving herself an out that way. With a sigh, she rejected that and got back to business. There had to be a hundred different ways to broach the subject and get it over with. Why was it that she couldn't think of any?

Focus! she ordered herself as she started walking back to her desk. Think! And once she started trying a little harder, ideas began to come to her. Not that any of them were any good. Still, she'd started the juices flowing.

There really were so many options. There was the blunt method. She could walk into his office, plunk a picture of the almost-fifteen-month-old twins down on the desk in front of him and say, "Look at these. See any resemblance?"

Dropping down into her chair, she made a face. A bit crass, perhaps. But it was a start. Leaning on her elbows, she frowned, deep in thought.

How about writing him a memo—make it businesslike? "Attention Mr. Carver: This memorandum is meant to inform you that you are the father of twins. Please deal with this situation immediately."

She wrinkled her nose.

Well then, how about using the office loudspeaker? "Attention employees. All fathers of twins please meet with Darcy Connors in the conference room right away. Mitch Carver, this means you."

A more subtle approach? "Uh, Mitch, you know when you left me in Paris? You didn't just leave me. In fact, you left behind a legacy, and it's been growing ever since."

Too obscure. He would think she meant the Parisian waitresses were still talking about him. And they just might be, but that wasn't the issue here.

She glanced at the clock and her heart jumped. She didn't have much time left. She had to think of some way to do this, fast, and do it right. Closing her eyes, she tried to concentrate. Her twins deserved a father who didn't completely reject them. And it was up to her to provide that for them. The way she approached this might make all the difference.

A few minutes later she was walking into his office and she still didn't have a plan. She did have a rough idea of what she might say, but she didn't get a chance to say it. Mitch rose from behind his desk to greet her, taking her hand in his and staring down into her eyes in a way that reminded her of how he'd looked in that Parisian doorway, blasting all thought right out of her mind and leaving only a thrilling electricity running through her veins and a bitter-sweet yearning in her heart.

"I've got to tell you right up-front, Darcy," he said, not releasing her hand. "I've talked to a few people and there's no chance to get your assignment changed. The only way we're going to avoid working with each other is if one of us quits."

She nodded numbly. She'd pretty much accepted that already. But he was still holding her hand and as long as he was doing that, her mind wasn't going to work very well. She gave a tug, but he wasn't letting go.

"I think I understand why you don't think we should be working together," he was saying earnestly. "But that's just it—I agree. You don't have anything to worry about. I swear, I'll make sure everything stays on a businesslike level. We'll work as colleagues and that will be it."

"Good," she said thickly. "Now can I have my hand back?"

He looked down and actually seemed startled to realize he was still holding it. "Oh. Sure. Sorry."

He let go and she took a step back to get a bit of distance from him and settle her emotions. If just having her hand in his was going to send her into a tailspin, she was in big trouble. She had to get control of herself.

Taking a deep breath, she stared at his tie and tried to get it together. Now was the time. They had the privacy she needed. There was a pause in the conversation. It was the perfect opportunity. She ought to launch into a speech that would prepare him for the revelation. She tried to make herself do it. Looking up into his face, she searched for the words.

If not now, when? she prodded herself silently. Come on. Get it out there.

CHAPTER THREE

DARCY opened her mouth. Her lips actually formed a word. But as she gazed up into his clear blue eyes, she just couldn't go through with it. The right words weren't there yet. They weren't coming to her.

"So what do you think?" Mitch asked, looking at her in the deep, probing way he had, that way that gave her the false feeling he saw only her, cared about only her, and would treasure her forever. "Can you work with me?"

"I...I don't know," she said, her voice sounding scratchy from the effort to speak at all. It was that intimate look that made her so crazy. She realized that now. She had to avoid his gaze at all costs. "That all depends. There's something..."

"We'll give it a try," he said when she faltered. "I'm sure we can do it. And it's only for one year."

One year! In one year, the twins would be talking. Talking? They would be writing novels! They would be learning to catch a ball. They would be giving wet baby kisses to the ones who loved them. Would that include Mitch?

"One year?" she repeated numbly.

He nodded. "That's all I've committed to. One year. And then I'm going back overseas."

"I see."

Well, wasn't that just typical? Full commitment wasn't his thing, was it? Resentment rose in her again.

"I…I guess I'm just surprised to see you working back here at all," she noted distractedly. "The last I heard you were smuggling arms into Nepal or something."

Amusement flashed across his handsome face. "Who told you that?"

"Someone at Jimmy's funeral, I think."

He shrugged, his gaze suddenly hooded. "He didn't get it quite right. It wasn't Nepal, and it wasn't arms."

"What was it?"

He paused just long enough to make her think whatever he said was going to be something he probably made up.

"It was rock concert T-shirts, into a country which shall remain nameless," he said at last. "I do still have my Fifth Amendment rights."

She barely restrained herself from rolling her eyes. "That you do, but you're the only person I've ever known who actually feels he needs to use them," she said a bit caustically.

"Actually we were just importing the shirts." He

paused, and then added softly, "And then 'exporting' a few political refugees."

"I see." She knew he was involved in dangerous things overseas. He'd told her a few hair-raising tales that night in Paris. And she was pretty sure the story behind that new ugly scar across his chest was going to fit right into one of those scenarios. "I guess you were just born to be a businessman, weren't you?" she added wryly.

He laughed softly. "Of a sort."

She bit her lip. Now *that* was something to keep in mind: Don't make the man laugh. He looks too good doing it.

"So is that why you're back?" she asked quickly. "Are you on the lam?" Where had that phrase come from? She didn't know, but she kind of liked it. It fit. "Is Interpol after you? I guess you got tired of being shot at and decided to come home for a rest, huh?"

He groaned, sagging down into a leather chair and stretching his long legs out before him. "You watch too much television."

"Then why *did* you come back?"

He looked up at her and smiled sweetly. "My mother asked me to."

She stared at him. *Because his mother asked him to?* That didn't fit in with the always-a-rebel, devil-may-care, to-hell-with-convention image she had of him. And now here he sat in a suit and tie—looking like he was ready to take the business world by storm.

It seemed his mother had a bigger influence on him than she'd thought.

Mitch's parents had been another dilemma for her. Her impulse had been to tell them about the twins soon after she'd known she was pregnant. The fact that Mitch was so adamant about wanting nothing to do with them was what had made her hesitate in the beginning.

And the more she thought about it, the more she wondered if she really wanted them getting involved in how she raised her children. Without knowing how things really stood with their son, did she dare let that happen? If there had been a different attitude, she might have told them.

But at first, she kept thinking Mitch would show up in one way or another. Or at least, that she would find a contact point. And that once she'd settled things with him, he should be the one to tell his parents.

She actually tried to talk to his mother at the company memorial service held for Jimmy. The woman had been gracious in a distant way, but when Darcy had tried to ask where Mitch was, she turned frosty fast.

"I'm sorry. I haven't talked to my oldest son for a long time," she said. "You'll have to find some other way to get in touch with him."

After that, she realized that if she went directly to the Carvers and told them about her pregnancy, they would immediately assume she was after money. She had to admit, a little financial aid would have come in very handy at that time. But once she'd thought things through, she knew it was just too dangerous. Money bought influence and got lawyers involved. It was much safer to take care of things herself.

That meant, sadly, that the Carvers were deprived of their grandchildren, and the twins were cheated out of grandparents, but she couldn't see a way around that at the time.

"So there's actually something you respect," she said slowly. "Your mother. That's sort of touching."

She'd meant it as a barb, but once the words were out of her mouth, she realized it was true.

"You're damn right I respect my mother. Have you met her?"

"Yes. She's a lovely woman."

"That she is."

She frowned, thinking back on the things he had told her almost two years before. "It was really your father you had the quarrel with, wasn't it?"

His face hardened. "That's something I'm not going to discuss."

Yes, she remembered now. All the bad feeling in the family revolved around some sort of feud with his father. And it obviously still burned deeply in him.

"You know, Darcy," he said, leaning back in his chair, "I didn't find out about what happened to Jimmy until just a few weeks ago." He frowned and muttered, "I really ought to go by and pay my respects to his mother. I always liked her."

Darcy nodded. Mimi was great. In fact, it was Mimi, Jimmy's mother, who had taken her in when she had the twins. She was living with her right now. Mimi had health problems and Darcy had two little babies who required looking after. They needed each other and they seemed to have the perfect fit, for now.

"You really have been out of touch, haven't you?" she noted. "How did your mother manage to find you?"

"She hired a private investigator."

So he hadn't even contacted the mother he claimed to be so close to. She frowned. This lack of family feeling did not bode well for his having any interest in the boys. But she'd known that all along.

"So all those things you said when we knew each other in…" She had force herself to say the name of the city. "In Paris…"

"Ah. You remember Paris, do you?" He pretended to be surprised.

She frowned, looking away. "Of course, I remember Paris."

"But you'd like to forget," he said softly, then grimaced. "Why do I get the feeling that what happened in Paris is looming over us like…like this giant vulture ready to pick apart the bones of our relationship?"

"Relationship?" she responded tartly. "Do we have a relationship? I thought that was one of those things you vowed never to have."

He sighed. "Tell you what, Darcy. I'll make you a deal."

Folding her arms, she looked at him sideways. "What sort of deal?"

"Look. Facing reality, we're probably going to be working together. It would be best if we could fix things so that's possible. So why don't we just put Paris behind us? That was then. This is now. We've both changed. Circumstances have certainly changed. A lot of water under the bridge." He shrugged. "Let's start over again. Completely new."

He rose and stuck out his hand. "Hi. I'm Mitch Carver. And I'm very pleased to meet you, Darcy Connors. I'm sure we'll work well together."

She stared at him and found her hand enveloped in his once again, but she couldn't join in the general good cheer he was trying to promote. Act as though Paris never happened? Sorry. There were two little impediments waiting for her at home that made all this impossible.

Still, his touch had power. She felt his energy, his inner strength, and especially, his raw, masculine appeal, just in the warmth of his hand. Her pulse began to race, as though something exciting was about to happen. Startled, she pulled her hand out of his.

"You are so arrogant," she told him gently, wishing she could will away his attractive presence. "You think you can wipe out the past, just by deciding to."

"Of course. Why not?"

She shook her head. "I think you still have a lot to learn," she said, regarding him narrowly.

Okay, she finally had a plan. She would think things over tonight, develop a method of attack, and give it to him in the morning. It would probably be best to do that somewhere outside of work. After all, she had no idea how he was going to react, but she did have a feeling it was going to be messy.

"Tell you what," she said, turning to go. "Meet me tomorrow morning at The Jumpin' Bean. You remember where that is, don't you? Seven-thirty. There's something I need to talk to you about."

He frowned, rising to see her out, his gaze suddenly alert. "What is it?"

She shook her head. "Tomorrow," she said. "Will you meet me?"

He shrugged. "Of course."

She nodded. "Okay. See you tomorrow."

And she left his office feeling a little better about the future. At least she had a plan.

"Look at that, boys," Mimi Foster announced in her slow Texas drawl. "Your mama's home!"

Darcy swept her two toddlers up in her arms, laughing as they babbled at her happily and Sparky, Mimi's little white fluffy dog, danced around her, barking noisily.

"Oh hush, Sparky," she said, and to her babies, "My little ducks, I'm so glad to see you." She cooed, kissing one and then the other and holding both tightly. "Have you been good for Mimi today?"

"They've been perfect angels, both of them," Mimi lied kindly. A tall, slender woman, she favored exotic caftans and chandelier earrings.

"Right. I'll just bet they have." Darcy sighed as she put them back down in the playpen. Looking around the tidy front room of the modest Spanish-style house she'd been sharing with Jimmy's mother since she'd come back to Terra Dulce in the San Antonio area, she shook her head. "Oh, Mimi, I don't know what I'd do without you."

"Darcy, darlin'," the older woman said, rising and giving her friend a hug. "You know the three of you are my family now. Without y'all I would just wither up and blow away."

Mimi and her mother had been best friends, and though they lived in cities hundreds of miles apart, there had been plenty of visits and vacations spent together. For years her mother and Mimi had planned and plotted, trying to conjure up a romance between Darcy and Jimmy that just never quite panned out. Jimmy had always been more interested in cars than he had in girls. And Darcy…well, Darcy had seen Mitch.

The first time she'd noticed him, she must have been about eleven. He was probably fourteen and full of teenage swagger. He'd stopped by the Foster house to help Jimmy work on an old car Jimmy's dad had in the driveway. Darcy's family had been there on their usual summer visit and she'd watched from the window. She thought most boys were "icky" at that point in her life. But Mitch was different. She couldn't take her eyes off him. From then on, Mitch was her standard for male excellence.

And now he was here and she was finally going to have to tell Mimi that he was the father of her children. She knew Mimi had hoped that Jimmy was their father at first. She'd let her know that wasn't the case, but she hadn't gone any further than that and Mimi hadn't tried to pry it out of her. The rest of the world, especially those she worked with, assumed Jimmy had been the father, and she hadn't done anything to counter that. When you came right down to it, she hadn't told anyone the full truth. And now, she had to find a way to tell Mitch.

She spent the next hour playing with her children and thinking about Mitch. Tonight she would take a long bath and work up a good way to present the facts to him. She had to phrase it just right. She had to let him know that she expected him to be a factor in their lives.

A part of her wished she could just grab her kids and make a run for it, start over somewhere fresh without all these problems. But she knew running just brought up new problems. And then the old ones came along and found you anyway.

Besides, it didn't seem likely she could get away in time, especially as, looking out the picture window, she saw Mitch coming up the front walk at this very moment. In seconds he would be knocking on the front door.

Sheer panic shot through her veins. Without thinking twice, she snatched up both babies, kicked the playpen behind the couch and whisked them into their bedroom before the doorbell rang. Her only hope was to move up naptime by an hour. Would these two little mop-heads cooperate?

"Mitch Carver! You darlin'!"

Mimi had answered the door and Darcy knew she was throwing her arms around the man who had been her son's childhood friend. Darcy listened intently as she put her babies down in their beds, hoping against hope they might take a nice nap. Maybe this could be quick. Maybe Mitch would just pay his respects and be on his way. Maybe Mimi would forget to mention that Darcy was living here with her.

Maybe.

"Mama," Sammy was saying sleepily, giving her a toothless smile. "Mama, Mama, Mama."

"Shush! Go to sleep, you little rascal," she whispered to him, love pouring out of her heart as she looked down at him.

Sean was already drifting off, his little thumb sneaking up into his mouth. No matter what, her total agenda was protecting these two adorable children from harm. She would do whatever she had to do.

She looked around the room and sighed. It was small for two cribs, one dresser and an ancient changing table, not to mention a shelf system that was beginning to pull away from the wall. This was not exactly what she'd dreamed of for her little ones. Hopefully, if she got the raise she was expecting next month…

"I wanted you to know how sorry I am about Jimmy," she could hear Mitch saying from the next room.

"His death was a tragedy," Mimi responded sadly. "You were always such a good friend to him. He idolized you, you know. He missed you so when you went off and joined the Army."

They chatted a bit more, but Darcy couldn't make out the words. Darcy bit her lip. So far, so good. Maybe he would just leave now, without ever hearing that she was just a few steps away.

"I don't know if you ever knew Darcy Connors," she heard Mimi mentioning, loud and clear.

"Darcy Connors?" Mitch sounded surprised. "Sure, I know Darcy."

Her shoulders sagged. Oh well. So much for that hope. Nothing was ever easy, was it? The boys were dozing. At least she was getting a little luck there. Very quietly, she crept out into the hall, ready to leap out and stop Mimi from bringing up the children if she possibly could.

"I was so happy when she got the assignment in France," Mimi was saying. "She and Jimmy became quite close while they were working together over there."

"I…yes, I guess I knew that," Mitch replied a bit stiffly.

Mimi was chattering on. Darcy crossed her fingers, hoping she would forget to mention the twins.

"Yes, she came to live with me right after she got transferred from the Atlanta office. And now she and her two—"

Time to make her move.

"Hello there," Darcy interrupted, bursting onto the scene with a bright smile before Mimi could get the rest of that sentence out. "I thought I recognized your voice," she said, nodding to Mitch.

He was firmly ensconced on the couch, unfortunately. She wasn't going to be able to shoo him out the door any time soon. Flopping down into a chair across from him, she kept on smiling.

He gave her a puzzled look and she knew he was wondering why she hadn't told him she was living with Jimmy's mom. *It just didn't come up,* she tried to convey with a subtle shrug.

Mimi was laughing about the past. "All those long summer days with you and Jimmy playing in the canyon out back, and me driving you to Little League games and buying you hamburgers at Merle's drive-in."

"Merle's Mammoth Mouthfuls." Mitch grinned. "I remember it all. Some of the happiest days of my life were spent right here in your backyard."

"You and Jimmy, what a pair." She sighed. "I'm

glad he had you in his life. And Darcy, too," she added with a smile. "I hope you two get to know each other."

Darcy and Mitch exchanged a quick, furtive glance.

"I haven't told Mimi yet," she said quickly.

"Told me what?" Mimi asked.

Mitch was staring at her, his eyes wide, as though he couldn't believe his ears, and she suddenly realized what he might think she was talking about.

"That we're going to be working together," she reassured him quickly. She turned to look at the older woman. "Yes, we're going to be working together, Mitch and I. He's come back and he's working for ACW. Isn't that nice?"

"Well, yes," Mimi said. "I'm so glad, Mitch. I know your mama must be pleased as punch. I haven't talked to her for years but she always seemed like a gracious lady."

Mitch looked as though he was still reeling from his brief misapprehension. How he had thought she was going to bring up the Paris incident she couldn't imagine. But it was pretty obvious he'd thought so, for just a moment there.

"Uh…yes, she is," he managed to get out.

Mimi smiled at them both. "So where did you two meet? How do you know each other so well?"

"I wouldn't say we know each other well," Mitch said hastily.

"No, not at all," Darcy echoed quickly.

"Well, what was it? You didn't just meet today, did you?"

Darcy smiled nervously. "Oh, no. We've met before."

She hesitated, glancing at Mitch and reading the wariness in his eyes. *Don't worry,* she wanted to tell him. *I'm not going to bring up Paris.* In fact, she was going to go back a lot further than that.

"Remember that summer, the first time my mother was sick and you invited me to come and stay with you?" she said to Mimi.

"You were still in high school."

"Yes. It was in August. You wanted to get my mind off my mother and all that. So I came to stay for a couple of weeks. You tried hard to get Jimmy to pay some attention to me, to take me out to where the teenagers gathered, but all he wanted to do was work on that souped-up car he loved so much."

"Of course! I remember." She smiled fondly. "I was so mad at him! He would barely give you the time of day. I guess it was a coming-of-age sort of thing with him."

No. It was the fact that he loved cars better than people. But that wasn't something she was going to point out to his mother.

"Anyway, you felt sorry for me, so one day you sent me off to the rodeo with a bunch of kids. Friends of Jimmy's."

"Did I?"

"Yes. I think that's the first time I really met Mitch." She glanced at him. He had the look of a man trying to remember details.

"I'd forgotten all about that," he said. "Was that really you?"

Their gazes met and something flashed between them, but Darcy ignored it as best she could. "That was me. I was the one who got charged by the bull that got out of the pen."

He grinned as the picture cleared for him.

"I remember that," he said as though enjoying the memory.

"And you pulled me out of his path at the very last second," she added. "My hero." She tried for a mocking tone but somehow it came out sounding almost sincere.

"I do my best," he said, managing to hit just the right note of irony, coming off modest and noble at the same time.

She shook her head, but she could have told him more. She could have told him that he really had become her hero that day. She could have recalled everything he was wearing, from the backward baseball cap to the tight muscle T-shirt and the ragged jeans. She might have recited everything he said to her, from, "Hey, watch it kid," to, "So you turned sweet sixteen yesterday, huh? I hope Jimmy kissed you. No? Well then, I guess I'll have to do it."

Even now, the memory of that silly little kiss could

curl her toes. But there was no way she would ever tell him that.

Oh, he remembered all right. She'd said something about it when they first met again in Paris and he'd acted like he didn't remember then. But she could see it in his eyes—he remembered now. The scene played out like a holograph between them— the two of them waiting for the others behind the stadium, the sounds and smells of the rodeo, the August evening heat, the way he'd grinned and tilted her chin up with a curved finger, then bent slowly to touch his warm lips to hers, the way the world had melted around them.

And then the others had come charging around the corner and they'd pulled apart. Mitch was quickly talking and laughing with his friends. But Darcy was in a dream, and she stayed there all the way home.

"So I suppose you'll both be working on the Heartland Project we've been reading so much about in the papers?"

Darcy's mind snapped back to the present. She and Mitch would be working on finishing up the Bermuda Woods assignment, but she knew it was possible it could flow seamlessly into this new project. She hadn't considered that before.

Mitch was looking at Mimi questioningly. "The Heartland Project? What's that?"

"You haven't heard of it? It's going to be huge. A

planned community out in the Sargosa Hills. The whole town is buzzing about it."

Mitch raised an eyebrow as he looked at Darcy. She nodded. "We're bidding on a portion of it. But I don't think Mitch and I will be working on it, except in a peripheral way. I'm sure the old-timers have dibs on it. People like Ned Varner," she added for emphasis, naming the senior vice president of the firm.

Mitch looked thoughtful and Darcy wondered what he was thinking. It would indeed be interesting if he decided he wanted to get in on the biggest project ACW had ever been involved in. If they did win the bid.

"Let me get you something to drink," Mimi was saying, rising expectantly. "Some nice iced tea? Some lemonade?"

Realizing what Mimi had said, Darcy's heart sank. If he accepted refreshment, he'd be here forever. But Mitch quickly revived her hope as he started rising from the couch.

"Oh, no. I'd really better get going. I just wanted to stop by and say 'hi'. And to let you know I'm around if you need anything."

Mimi reached out and warmly took his hand. "I hope you'll come by and see us often."

His smile to her was just as warm. "I will."

Darcy sprang up. Inside, she was exalting. He was going! Great. All she needed was some time to get her thoughts together. Tomorrow he would know the truth.

"Yes, well, it's been awfully nice seeing you."

She pulled open the door and smiled, waiting for him to make his way out onto the porch, mentally urging him forward.

And for just a moment, it looked like she was going to get her wish. He started toward the door. As he came even with where she was standing, he looked at her sideways. She gave him a tiny shrug and he shook his head just enough for her to see. She wanted to reach out and plant the palm of her hand between his shoulder blades and push him out the door, but she resisted, gritting her teeth with the effort. He was almost gone.

And then Mimi spoiled it all.

"Well, wait a minute," she said, frowning. "You can't go yet. You haven't even met the babies."

CHAPTER FOUR

DARCY froze, holding her breath.

"Babies?" Mitch was saying, just the way she'd imagined he would. "What babies?" He looked thunderstruck.

"Darcy's two little ones, of course," Mimi said. "The twins. Didn't you know?"

He turned back into the room. His gaze met hers.

"You've got babies?" He said it as though he was sure there had to be some sensible answer to this puzzle, hopefully one he could accept.

"Bring them out, Darcy," Mimi was urging. "Let Mitch see them."

She licked her dry lips. This was not the right way to do it. "Uh, they're sleeping."

"Already?" Mimi looked skeptical. "You just put them in there. How did you get them to sleep so fast?"

"Magic powers?" she quipped, still hanging on to her last shred of hope.

The sound of a crash came from the bedroom, and hope was gone.

"Noisy sleepers," Mitch said dryly, his steel-colored eyes penetrating. "I'm guessing your powers aren't quite what you thought they were."

Darcy managed a tremulous smile, then turned on her heel and headed for the bedroom to see what had happened. Mimi and Mitch were close behind her. There was no way to stop this now. He was going to see the boys. And what was he going to see when he looked into their blue eyes, so like his own? Was he going to recognize parts of himself staring back at him? And if he did, what was he going to do about it? Apprehension shivered through her.

She opened the bedroom door to reveal a scene of minor chaos. Somehow, Sammy had gotten out of the crib and made his way to the changing table, which he had tried to climb, knocking down the baby powder, which landed on his head. There he sat on the floor, covered with powder and grinning broadly, very pleased with himself. Meanwhile Sean sat in his own crib, looking through the bars at his brother and laughing with a silly hiccuping sound. Sammy tried to clap his hands. He missed, but he did manage to send up a cloud of baby powder, making Sean laugh even harder.

"He climbed out!" Darcy cried, looking at the extra-high bars she'd paid extra for. "How did he do that?"

"Oh my," Mimi said, shaking her head. "How

could one little boy do so much damage in such a short time?"

It took a few moments and Mimi's help to get things back in order. Darcy murmured a few stern words, then a few more soft reassurances to Sammy as she cleaned him up and then safely installed him back in bed. In the meantime she'd forgotten all about Mitch standing there, watching it all, until she turned and saw him leaning against the doorjamb.

Meeting his gaze, she tried to read what he was thinking from the look in his eyes, but his gaze was hard, hooded. She deliberately lifted her chin. She was proud of these little guys and she wanted to show that.

"Mitch, this is Sammy and this is Sean. My boys." She made a flourish and waited to see what he would say.

Mitch was numb. This changed everything. Darcy had children. Twin boys. And they looked way too familiar for comfort.

His first thought was that these must be Jimmy's children. After all, Darcy was living here with Jimmy's mother. It seemed logical. But there was a problem with that theory. He couldn't remember exactly what color eyes Jimmy had, but he was pretty sure they weren't blue. Darcy had eyes that flashed almost ebony. And these little boys had the bluest eyes he'd ever seen—outside of his own baby pictures. In fact, these babies could have been stand-ins for him and his brother.

He turned and looked at Darcy. She looked at him. There was an air of defiance in her face. He felt like he couldn't pull a breath in all the way.

"We need to talk," he said softly.

She nodded.

"Why didn't you want me to know?" he asked her bluntly as soon as they were far enough away from the house to speak freely.

Biting her lip she kept her head down. They were walking between two houses, heading for the open area of scrub pine that lined the canyon that ran just north of the neighborhood. Mimi had agreed to watch the babies for a while, to give them time to take a walk.

"I was going to tell you tomorrow, when we went for coffee," she said, wishing it didn't sound like an excuse.

He shook his head, rejecting her statement. "I don't know, Darcy. You weren't acting like someone who wanted to come clean." There was a real flash of anger in his voice. "You don't contact me for two years. You move to the place you know I've sworn I'll never go to again. When I show up, you act cagey." He turned to face her. His eyes were troubled and the muscles of his neck stood out like cords. "I don't buy it. You didn't want me to know."

She stopped and stared up at him, mouth open with astonishment. "What are you talking about? You're the one who stepped out into a crowd in Paris and never looked back. You might as well have stepped off the face of the earth. You certainly disappeared from my life without a second thought. I…I tried for months to find you."

She paused to steady her voice. She wasn't going to let emotions take over and the last thing in the world she wanted to do was cry.

"That had to be a very deliberate disappearing act to let you vanish so completely," she pointed out.

"You knew where I was going."

"Oh sure. Brazil." She threw up her hands and started walking again, mostly so she wouldn't have to look into his eyes. "It's a big country. But I suppose I could have called up the Brazilian phone company and asked to be connected to that tall, handsome American who went by various names but might have entered the country as Mitch Carver." She flashed a scathing look over her shoulder. "I'm sure they would have found you right away."

He sighed, shoving his hands down into his pockets. "Okay, I guess I wasn't the easiest person to find at the time," he admitted gruffly, his long stride keeping pace with her quick steps. "But you knew the kind of work I do. You knew I was going to be melting into other cultures. I told you what my life was like."

"You did. And that's fine. I can understand that."

She could understand it on a certain level. But she couldn't forgive the fact that he hadn't felt the need to contact her in any way. Had he forgotten her the moment he'd stepped on the plane? Had the time they spent together, time that had changed her life for good, been so meaningless to him? Was she just another woman in a string of affairs? Her heart cracked when she thought that way.

"I understand that you can't be tied down," she was saying. "I never really expected that of you. Not while I was sane, at any rate," she added, letting a note of sarcasm creep into her tone. "And I don't expect it now."

He swore softly, shaking his head. "What I don't get is, what made you so sure...?"

"That they're yours?" She swung around to face him, her eyes glittering. "I can't believe you could ask such a thing!"

He stared at her. "Darcy, I didn't ask it. I can see they're mine. You don't have to prove anything to me."

"Oh. Well, good." Her cheeks filled with color and heat, but the relief that also filled her blotted out any embarrassment. She hadn't really let herself formulate the fear, but now she knew she'd been dreading that he would want explanations and promises. And if he had demanded those things, she was ready to hate him.

As if that were possible.

Well, anyway, she'd been planning to be really, really angry. Only now, she didn't have to be. That left her with an empty space inside, but it quickly filled up with more yearning. She just couldn't help it. Even when she was angry with him, she couldn't turn off the feelings that surged in her when she looked at him.

They reached the edge of the canyon and both stopped, looking down at the sharp drop off into wild brush. Mitch's mind went back for a moment to when he and Jimmy had spent hours in all that wilderness as boys, losing themselves in adventure fantasies. He hadn't realized at the time that he would grow up to live some of those playacting scenes out in real life. He kicked at a rock and listened as it skittered down the side of the canyon, until it got lost in the underbrush.

"I guess we weren't as careful as we should have been, were we?" he mused, remembering that for the short amount of time they'd spent together, there had been an awful lot of chances to forget to be careful. Once they'd begun, they'd both been insatiable—probably because they knew they had so little time. What else could have made them so crazy?

"So what now?" he asked gruffly. "Do we get married, or what?"

"Oh!"

She let the small word out with so much outrage, he looked up in surprise. He was only trying to figure out what was expected in situations like this. He'd never been here before. Was he supposed to know everything?

"I wouldn't marry you if you were…" She clamped her lips shut, cutting off the cliché, but they both knew it by heart. She took a deep breath. "Let me put it this way," she said more carefully. "There are men who are fathers, and there are men who are biological donors." She glared at him. "We'll just put you into the latter category, okay? You've made your most important contribution. Now all we need from you is health information and maybe an occasional financial donation. And that, only when absolutely necessary."

He frowned. He didn't like the way she was putting things, but right now, he hadn't thought the situation through well enough to know what he wanted to say in rebuttal. Still, he did know he didn't want to shirk his duty in any way.

"Listen, Darcy, I agree that a marriage between you and me just wouldn't work out, but I definitely want to help you in any way I can. We need to figure how much money you'll need and I'll set up a monthly fund."

"No!"

She was cringing inside. How was it that he didn't understand that his offer was so hurtful she could hardly bear it—that it was even worse than his half-hearted mention of marriage that seemed so easy to brush away? That it was so obvious he just wanted to get the hell out of here. She closed her eyes, but only for a few seconds. She couldn't let herself weaken.

"I will take some help because I'm going to need it," she said, her voice rough as she tried to rein in her emotions. "But only enough to make sure the twins are okay." She drew in a deep breath. "But help is one thing. Taking over my life is another."

"Who said anything about taking over your life?"

She stared down into the canyon. "Those who give money always end up seeking control. It's human nature."

And then she wanted to bite her tongue. Why was she being so testy? This bristling edginess between them seemed so strange. They'd never been this way with each other before. In the old days, when he'd hardly glanced her way, she'd watched from afar, thinking he was the most wonderful thing in the world.

And then there had been Paris. The attraction between them had been immediate and explosive— a match being struck and igniting into instant flame. The joy of being together in that beautiful city, the ecstasy of the love they'd made in that narrow bed in his tiny hotel room, walking together down the wide boulevard and watching the dawn arrive over the spires and treetops of the sleeping city—it had all been a magical fantasy that she would cherish forever.

But that was then. This was reality, where they were giving each other scathing looks and tight-lipped smiles and acting as though they could barely stand to look at each other. What had happened? Was it just because of the babies?

She tried to imagine what it would have been like if there were no children, if he'd come back and found her much the way he'd left her. But no, it wouldn't be very different. Even without the babies, there was still the fact that he'd walked off and forgotten all about her in a few short moments after that weekend. And she'd been able to think about nothing else—until Jimmy's accident took center stage in her life. After all, when their eyes had first met in that washroom, there had been no spontaneous burst of joy between them. To the contrary, there had been an instant antagonism, an instant wariness—and it hadn't been just her.

Face facts, Darcy, she told herself bitterly. He's a love 'em and leave 'em guy who doesn't particularly care to find the ones he's left turning up on his doorstep. That much is obvious.

"Who knows about this?" he was asking.

"That you are their father? Nobody." She shrugged. "Nobody but you and me. And I think Mimi is probably figuring it out as we speak."

He nodded. "Okay. Do you want to leave it that way?"

No, of course she didn't. But what else could she say? She turned so that he couldn't see her face.

"I guess so. Especially since we're going to be working together. I think it would be best, don't you?"

He nodded again.

She looked back at him. "You might want to tell your parents."

His handsome face registered surprise. "Why would I do a thing like that?"

"They're grandparents and don't even know it. Don't you think they have a right to know?"

Slowly he shook his head. "They have nothing to do with my private life."

"Oh." She searched his face, puzzled by his attitude. His tone was so bitter. "I've met your father. I think he's a very nice man."

"Most people do."

She rolled her eyes, just a little. "I see. Those who don't know him like you do."

"You've got that right."

She frowned, shaking her head and searching his face for clues. "What did he do to you, Mitch?" she asked gently.

Something hard flashed in his gaze and he grimaced. "We're off topic," he said. "We were talking about the fact that you had two kids who are part mine and you didn't tell me about it."

She lifted her chin. "No. We're talking about the fact that I had two kids who are part yours and you wish I hadn't."

He stared down at her. How could he deny what she'd just said? It was true. She'd dropped a bombshell on him and he hadn't recovered from the impact yet. He really wasn't sure what he thought.

But one thing he knew for sure—babies or not, life-changing news or not, antagonism or not—he still wanted her like he'd never wanted any other woman. Every time he looked at her he felt that same pull, an attraction so strong, so deep, that it seemed almost physical. She drew him like a magnet. He longed for her, ached to hold her, hungered to feel that open, unrestrained response she'd given him in Paris. And yet, that seemed to be more and more impossible every moment. He could almost see the gulf widening between them. He hated that, but he had no idea how to stop it.

He'd been in a state of denial. He realized now that he'd felt this way for a long time. He'd dreamed about her on cold, empty nights in the Himalayas, seen her face in the reflective glass of windows on the streets of Brasilia, thought about her when he was alone and when he was in crowds. She'd been haunting him for two years. No wonder he'd finally had to come back.

But that didn't make any sense. He hadn't known she'd be here. He shook his head, rejecting that random thought. And yet…

Now, suddenly, the woman who obsessed him was the mother of his children. That brought him up short. What was he supposed to do with that? Emotions were churning inside him but he needed to sort them out. He wasn't sure what he thought, what he felt. He needed a little time to think it all over.

"Listen, Darcy," he said, turning to head back toward the house. "This has really knocked me for a loop. I can't seem to put together a coherent thought right now. I need some time."

She nodded. They walked back in silence, the crunching of the rocks beneath their feet the only sound. A cool breeze was kicking up, slapping her blond hair against her face. She shivered and drew her arms in close. As they came back in front of the house, she turned to him. Despite everything, she longed to have him love the boys the way she did. Maybe, if he got to know them...

"Do you want to come in?"

"No."

She drew back, startled at his abrupt tone of voice.

"No," he repeated, deliberately sounding gentler this time. "I think I'd better go. I've got to think about this."

She nodded, but her heart sank. He seemed to read her disappointment in her face, because he hesitated and added, "Darcy, you know I'm not used to this yet. You've had two years to get used to it. I'm just starting down that road."

"Sure," she said. "I understand."

He raked fingers through his hair and looked at her with a half smile. "Do you? That's good. Because I sure don't."

She could have used a sharp retort against him but she didn't. Something in the lost, bewildered look in his eyes stopped her. He really had been sent into a tailspin and needed to right himself before they talked more. She could see that. So she nodded when he said, "Goodbye."

"See you tomorrow," she said simply.

She watched him get into his car and start down the driveway. She stood where she was until he was out of sight.

"Why me?" she whispered to whatever power in the universe might be listening. "Surely there are others who deserve to be tortured much more than I do."

This was all so disturbing, but she thought she understood him to a point. Yes, she understood his need for time to think, but there was something she didn't understand. Or, maybe she understood it too well and just didn't like it. He didn't want to come in and see the babies again. Maybe he would never want to see them. That thought was like a knife through her heart. How could he turn his back on those two sweet babies?

And yet, what did she expect him to do? Oh sure, he could write a check and pretend that took care of everything. But what else did she want from him? It wasn't even clear to her yet. Something was bruised deep inside her and she tried to figure out just exactly why. She was hurt and disappointed that Mitch was acting like he didn't want the babies, but this was more. This had to do with his reaction to *her.*

Maybe it was for all she'd lost. She wasn't that girl anymore, that open and loving woman who'd clung to him and made love to him so freely, so full of joy.

That girl was gone forever. She could no longer do things just because she wanted to. She had two little babies to care for. She had to take them into account before she did anything at all.

So maybe that was it—a sense of mourning for the lost Darcy of old.

"Whatever," she muttered to herself. "Good riddance, anyway."

But her eyes brimmed with tears.

"Has he gone?" Mimi asked as she came back into the house.

"Yes," Darcy answered. "Thanks for taking the babies for me. Are they down?"

"Yes indeed, and sleeping soundly. They were all worn out from their escapade."

Darcy smiled.

"Mitch is such a nice fellow," Mimi went on, bending to pick up a toy lodged halfway under the couch. "He was always one of my favorites of Jimmy's friends. Even with that mother of his."

"His mother? Do you know her well?"

"Not well, but of course we had to deal with each other over the years, our sons being friends and all." She stopped and considered, head to the side. "I always had the feeling that she wished Mitch would find someone else to spend his time with, someone from the wealthy neighborhood they lived in. But that could have been my imagination, I suppose."

Darcy nodded. "I had a similar feeling the day I tried to talk to her about getting in touch with Mitch."

"Oh. I see."

She saw everything and knew everything. Darcy shook her head, half laughing. "Oh, Mimi, the answer is yes, Mitch is the father of my babies."

Mimi shook her head, looking bemused. "Well, come on into the kitchen and have a cup of tea with me," she said, "and tell me all about it. This is a story that's been a long time coming, so it better be good."

Darcy laughed lovingly as she turned to follow her friend. She knew Mimi was still disappointed that she and Jimmy hadn't clicked romantically, but she was bighearted enough to want the best for Darcy anyway. And for the babies.

"It's a fairly short story," she warned. "But I'll see what I can do to embellish it for you."

"You do that," Mimi said approvingly. "And I'll brew the tea."

CHAPTER FIVE

IT HAD been three long days since Mitch had returned. He and Darcy had been working together for two of them, and he hadn't said a word about the twins. She'd started out on pins and needles, jumping every time he came near, waiting for him to bring up her babies and get things settled between them. But he was acting for all the world as though that afternoon at Mimi's had never happened. And she was rapidly losing patience with him.

"Why didn't you want me to know?" he'd said to her accusingly.

Well, Mitch, maybe this was why. Maybe it was because I knew you wouldn't react the way I wanted you to react. Maybe it was because you're just a big jerk.

Not really. After all, how could she criticize him for acting right in line with the way he'd warned her. He didn't want kids, didn't want to be tied to one woman, or tied down in Texas. So what did she expect?

Still, she came into work resolved on the fourth day. This was the day. It was time. She was going to confront him, get everything out in the open, make sure they each knew where they stood. She'd pumped herself up. She was ready to make him deal with the situation.

Sitting down at her desk, she was a model of fierce determination, drumming her fingers on the heavy wood and waiting for him to show his face.

And then she heard the laughter in the hallway. Turning, she beheld the spectacle of Mitch being escorted into the office suite by a bevy of the building's most attractive young women, all seemingly in a party mood. They giggled and called out teasing suggestions as they left him, and he looked very pleased with himself as he waved them off.

As the elevator doors closed on the last of them, he turned back to favor Darcy with a crooked grin. His tie was pulled open, as was the neck of his crisp white shirt. There were lipstick marks on his cheek and neck. His blue eyes were dancing with pure male happiness.

"Good morning," he said.

She couldn't respond. Something was choking her.

"Uh...sorry I'm a little late," he added, shrugging with boyish helplessness. "Some of the girls asked me to come in early for a meeting. I didn't realize they were planning a little surprise 'welcome back' party for me."

"I see," she managed to get out, and darned frostily, too.

But it was no use pretending. All her confidence was draining away, as though someone had pulled the plug on her reservoir. She didn't need to be reminded of what an attractive man he was. Women responded to him the way flowers turned toward the sun. It was a natural phenomenon she couldn't have stopped if she'd wanted to. She knew he had a thousand other options besides dealing with her and her twin boys.

So where was this confrontation she'd been planning? He walked on into his inner office, whistling tunelessly, and she closed her eyes. No confrontation, no settling of things. What was she trying to prove, anyway? If he wanted to be a part of her life, he would have said so by now. If he had any interest in the babies, he would have asked about them, or come by to see them. She couldn't make him care. If it wasn't there, it just wasn't going to be and she might as well face it.

Hurt and anger simmered inside her, but she tamped them down. She had work to do, and luckily, a reason to get out of the office and leave all this behind for most of the day. She had a few loose ends to attend to and then she was off on a field trip—and as far away from Mitch as she could get in one business day. The trick would be to avoid him and get out of here before he knew she was going.

Working quickly, she spent the next hour clearing up the work left over from the day before. She was almost ready to leave when she heard him coming back out of his office and she started typing furiously, concentrating like a laser beam on her work. Maybe he would notice how busy she was and go on by. She could always hope.

"Ah, Darcy," he said, almost as though he hadn't already seen her that morning. "There you are."

She sighed. Oh well. Looking up, she threw him a glance with the hint of a glare.

"You're right," she said tartly. "Here I am. Just like always. On time and with my wits about me." She stacked a few folders as though that was a very important thing to do right now.

He stood right over her and she didn't have to look up to know he was smiling. She knew he actually enjoyed it when she didn't play the docile employee. Why did she keep providing him with red meat this way? She couldn't seem to help herself.

Though they'd been working together for days now, she'd managed to avoid too much direct contact. Luckily he'd been spending a lot of time in meetings. Even luckier, the requirements of her job kept her out of the office a lot of the day. She was planning to do as much fieldwork as possible from now on.

"I'll agree you've got a strange sense of humor about you," he was saying. "But wits? We'll see."

He was trying to make a joke, trying to lighten the mood between them. But she didn't want it lightened. She made another careful pile of folders.

"I'm busy," she said without looking up.

"As usual," he noted. "But maybe you can spare me a minute or two."

She finally raised her head and reluctantly met his gaze. She'd been right. He was silently laughing at her.

"What can I do for you?" she asked with as much regal chill as she could manage.

"You can type up these meeting notes for me." He waved pages of yellow paper with a lot of things scribbled on them in her direction. "Okay?"

She looked at them. Her impulse was to grab them and start typing away. After all, it wouldn't really take all that long. But she stopped herself. She had to guard against letting him put her into a role she didn't deserve. So instead of accommodating him, she flashed him a look and shook her head.

"No, actually, I can't. Give them to Paula."

"She's out this morning."

"She'll be back."

"Maybe."

He still stood there, waving the papers at her.

She glared at him. "I guess I need to remind you again. I'm not a typist."

He frowned as though he didn't understand the word. "You're not a what?"

"A typist." She rose and opened a drawer, pulling out her little molded purse. It was obvious he thought she was being silly, but she didn't care. She'd worked hard to achieve her position and she wasn't going to let him discount it.

"I'm also not a secretary. I'm not even an administrative assistant. In fact, if you think about it really hard, I'm sure you'll recall that I'm a property acquisitions agent."

She tucked the purse under her arm and started toward the elevator, looking back at him over her shoulder.

"And I'm off to do some acquiring work right now. In fact, I'm late for a meeting with a contractor on the Pearson Development. So if you'll excuse me…"

He was following her, looking interested. "You're meeting with him right now?"

"Yes. I'm going out to Shadow Ridge."

"Great. I'll go with you."

Stopping dead, she swung around to face him. "What?"

He shrugged, looking remarkably handsome and civilized now that he'd wiped off the lipstick and straightened out his dark blue suit and the silver-blue tie. "Why not? I've got to get to know more about this business. You can show me the ropes."

She sagged. The last thing she needed was to spend the day carting him around and feeling resentful while doing it. "But Mitch…"

He was taking no arguments. "Look, Darcy. I'm like someone who's been dropped out of the sky here. I mean, I know I used to work here part-time when I was in high school and college, but I never paid much attention. I only wanted to get out of this town as soon as I could. On the whole, you know a lot more about this business right now than I do. If I'm going to do a decent job, I've got to learn. You can teach me."

She was supposed to teach him all she knew? Hah! That would be the day. She'd come by her knowledge the hard way, and he could do the same. Still, she couldn't deny him a seat in her car. If only there was some way she could talk him out of coming with her.

"You're going to miss lunch," she warned him hopefully.

"Lunch." He narrowed his eyes speculatively. "Are you talking about those cardboard slices of bread with some kind of fish substance slathered between them that they sell in the break room vending machine? Hmmm. Yes, that is a lot to give up just so that I can ride out into the warm sunny day to a rural area and listen to builders talk building. But sacrifices must be made." He gave her a lopsided grin that was, unfortunately, totally endearing. "Besides, we can grab something on the road. A hamburger maybe."

Folding her arms over her chest, she frowned, feeling sulky. "I don't 'grab things on the road.'"

He smiled, leaning across her to press the button for the elevator. "Don't worry. There's nothing to it. I'll show you how."

"Oh brother!"

"Besides," he said, his smile fading and eyes darkening seriously as he leaned close to say it softly, "we have some things to talk about. This will give us a chance to do that."

Her heart began to thump in her chest. So he wasn't going to ignore their situation after all. Well, good. Maybe. But just the fact that he thought they could discuss things on the fly given an odd moment or two didn't bode well. You just didn't make life commitments that way, did you?

As they hit the highway and left city traffic behind them, her anxiety began to melt away. How could she stay tense when that big ole Texas sky was shockingly blue and almost cloudless above them? There was something irresistible about an open road. She relaxed, her hands loose on the wheel.

Mitch had been quiet since they'd left the parking garage. Glancing at him sideways, she wondered what he was thinking. Was he preparing what he wanted to say to her? Or was he still mulling things over? Why didn't he just go ahead and get it over with? She had a feeling it must be really bad if he couldn't just spit it out on the spot.

Now she was getting tense again. This was no good.

"What kind of music do you like?" she asked, suddenly wanting something to fill the silence between them.

"You choose."

She hesitated. "Well, are you still Texan enough to take in a little country and western? Or have you become too cosmopolitan and sophisticated for us hayseeds?"

"Am I still Texan?" He turned toward her, appalled by the question. "Is the Pope Catholic?"

She refused to give him a smile. "Last time I looked."

"There's your answer." He snorted. "Am I Texan?" he repeated, and for good measure, he sang her a few lines from, a popular song, finally coaxing a smile from her.

"Not bad," she had to admit. "You're a man of many talents, aren't you?"

He laughed softly. "Darcy, I have only just begun to reveal myself to you."

She shook her head but she knew he was still feeling a bit full of himself after the way all those women had treated him that morning. He stretched out his long legs as best he could in the confinement of the car, and suddenly she was very much aware of him as a man—a man with a hard, gorgeous body, which she remembered only too well. She caught her breath as memories flooded her for a moment, pictures of his golden form stretched out on white sheets in lamplight.

Oh my. She hadn't thought of that for ages—and she really should block those things out of her mind, if she possibly could. She started to reach to turn up the air-conditioning, then caught herself just in time. But she couldn't stop the heat from flooding her cheeks, and she was only glad he seemed too occupied with the passing landscape to notice.

"You know, Darcy, you've got a few surprising facets to your persona as well," he said a few minutes later, turning toward her again. "It was a real shock to find out you had… the twins." His voice deepened. "I have to admit, though I thought of you often over the last two years, I never pictured you as a mother."

Well, that was just downright annoying. Sure, she was a mother. But that very fact made him a father. He seemed to be forgetting that part.

"I never thought of you as a Texas businessman," she shot back. "So we're even."

He frowned. "I'm not a Texas businessman," he protested.

"No?"

"Not really. Only temporarily."

"Well, cleaned up like you are, you could pass for one."

"Gee, thanks."

"Don't mention it."

They were silent for a moment, then he spoke again.

"So what *did* you think of me as?" he asked curiously.

She raised an eyebrow. "Fishing for compliments?"

"Not at all. Just curious."

She hesitated. What had she thought that day when she'd opened the door to Jimmy's pied-à-terre and found the hunky hero from her teenage years standing there in the Paris rain? He was exactly what any woman would have conjured up for herself if she'd had a magic wand. But what had come to mind at the time?

"An adventurer I guess." That wasn't exactly it, but the best she could come up with on short notice.

"An adventurer." He said the word as though that startled him, as though he wasn't sure he liked it.

"That's not the way you see yourself?"

He shook his head, looking distracted. "No. Actually I see myself more as a human rights worker."

She looked at him in astonishment, then had to swerve back into her lane. A human rights worker? And here she'd thought he was some sort of modern day mercenary. Maybe they had different ways of defining that term.

"You're kidding. Right?"

He sighed. "Never mind. For now, I guess I'm a businessman."

"So that's for sure, is it?" she asked, turning onto a smaller two-lane road. "You're saying that this return to your home town isn't permanent? That it's just something temporary in order to make your mother happy for a while?"

That seemed to offend him. "Leave my mother out of this," he said gruffly.

She looked at him in surprise. After all, he was the one who had originally brought the subject up. She hadn't realized it was out of bounds.

But he seemed to recognize what she was thinking.

"Sorry," he said. "I'm sort of defensive about my mother right now. I'm feeling a little protective."

Mitch protective toward his mother. She'd thought rebelling against his family situation had been the whole point. That was the impression she'd had from what he'd told her in Paris. Obviously she didn't have a handle on the full picture.

She pulled the car into the parking lot at the construction site. The twin mobile trailers, which served as the administration and engineering offices, sat in front of where they'd parked. Switching off the engine, she turned to look at the man beside her.

"I'm not sure why you came back," she told him candidly, "but since you did, we need to settle the business about the twins. We can't leave it up in the air the way it is now. Just what is your role going to be in their lives?"

He didn't answer right away, but he was studying her face, his gaze sliding over her lips, her nose line, her smooth skin, then tucking into the protected area around her ear. When his gaze finally rose to meet hers, she saw a sort of storminess there. But only for a moment.

"We'll talk," he promised. "Later today. Right now, we've got work to do." He turned away and reached to open the door. "Let's get this show on the road."

She followed more slowly, wondering what she was going to do with this man who wanted her to "show him the ropes." She should resent him, but somehow she just couldn't do that. Still, she had to be careful. "Give him an inch and he'll take a mile," she whispered to herself, shaking her head. That was just it. Keep track of your inches!

It was over an hour later when they emerged from the trailers. Darcy was feeling a bit shell-shocked. The meeting had started as usual. She and the contractor had gone over some figures and discussed a timetable. She'd brought up a few minor issues she'd had problems with and he tried to smooth over her concerns. All the while, Mitch had watched silently. And then he asked a question about the Heartland Project.

It was like he'd lit a fuse. The contractor seemed to take his question as a challenge, and before Darcy knew what was happening, the two men were shouting at each other and arguing about things she thought were pointless. She tried to intervene, but they didn't seem to hear her. They argued sharply, then came to an agreement about something. What it was she couldn't have said.

Then, as quickly as it had started, the firestorm was over. The two men had found a point in common and were talking like—well, maybe not old friends, but old acquaintances, at least. And as they left the trailer, the contractor shook her hand warmly and told her he would take care of all her little items, no problem.

"Thanks, Darcy," Mitch was saying as they

walked back toward the car. "I learned a lot." He grinned. "I especially learned that I'd better leave the talking to you whenever possible."

"On that point," she said, sliding in behind the wheel, "I think I agree."

He glanced over as she started the engine. In truth, he'd been impressed by the way she'd handled herself. She was good at what she did, good at talking to contractors, good at holding her own when the going got tough. Funny how that opened a whole new side of her to him, a side he'd never thought about during that weekend in Paris.

But it didn't change anything. It didn't help him to get over this weird fascination. He still wanted her with a deep, throbbing ache that wouldn't go away, no matter how much he tried to ignore it.

He'd spent the last two days trying to figure out a way this was going to work. At first he'd thought maybe he would get used to having her around all day. After all, there were plenty of other beautiful women at ACW. Just that morning he'd flirted with a lot of them. Unfortunately, as pleasurable as it had been to be lionized by a group of lovely ladies, he'd found himself looking at his watch and wondering whether Darcy had come in to work yet long before his welcome party was over.

Which just went to prove that this situation was impossible. He couldn't work with her. It was slow torture to see her and not be able to touch her. He looked at her now as she turned onto the highway. She was wearing a short, tailored skirt that rode up enough to display a nice view of her gorgeous legs. Just watching the interplay of muscles as she worked the accelerator made his blood begin to race a little faster.

It was a bittersweet reaction that came up all the time. A part of him reveled in his instant response to this woman, and another part rejected it, trying to turn it back before it caused him to make another mistake.

But it still happened every time she walked past him and he caught a hint of her fresh, sweet scent, every time she spoke to someone else in the outer office and he sat with his eyes closed listening to her cool, rich voice, every time she got up from her desk and he watched surreptitiously as she walked away toward the elevator, her silky hair rippling sensually, her round little bottom swaying impertinently, while sweet desire surged in his body, and cold, hard reproach stirred in his brain. No other woman had ever played with both his mental and physical response the way Darcy Connors did. He loved it and hated it at the same time.

And that was why he should be working to get her out of his daily life.

"How close are we to the perimeter of the Heartland Project?" he asked suddenly, realizing they must be passing near it.

She looked at him sideways. "There's a pullout at that hill ahead that gives a pretty good overview of the eastern boundary," she said. "I've got a pair of binoculars in the glove compartment."

"Great. Let's stop and take a look."

"Sure."

She pulled off the highway at the viewing area, rolling up to the thick guardrails.

"Here we are," she noted.

"Great," he said. "I really want to get a good look at this." He gazed at her earnestly. "But first I want to talk about our situation for a minute."

She threw him a startled look, but she did as he suggested, turning off the engine and turning toward him in the car. She didn't say a word, waiting for him to take the lead.

"Okay, here's the deal," he said firmly, determined not to show how mixed his feelings were about her. "We can't deny that we made two children together. And of course that it's as much my problem as yours."

She reacted as though he'd attacked her. "My babies are not a *problem*!"

He frowned, regretting his wording. "Darcy, relax. I didn't mean it that way exactly."

She was glaring at him. "Obviously they are a problem for you."

He sighed, not sure how they'd gotten off to such a bad start so quickly. "That's really not fair, Darcy. You knew from the beginning that my life was going to be nomadic. That I never expected to have a wife or kids because I couldn't be fair to them. I never pretended otherwise."

She took a deep breath and nodded. "I know," she said softly, her tone almost as good as an apology.

"Okay. Listen, first of all I want to commend you for having the babies. I know that's easy for me to say, not being with you or even knowing it was happening at the time. You went through it all by yourself for nine months. I can't tell you how sorry I am. And how much I admire you for it."

"It was a beautiful period of my life," she said somewhat defensively. There had been plenty of not-so-beautiful things about it, of course, but she wasn't going to whine about them.

"That may be," he said. "But I know it was hard."

She bit her lip. If he kept being so nice about things, she would start to cry. Her eyes were already stinging and she knew what that meant, but she refused to let it happen. She would not cry in front of him! If tears came she was going to jump out of the car and throw herself over the edge and into the canyon.

Well, not really. But thinking that gave her the strength to hold back the emotions that tried to overwhelm her.

"So, tell me this," he went on, staring out at the plains stretching out away from their position instead of looking her in the eye. "Why didn't you put them up for adoption?"

A sense of shock, very near horror, shot through

her. Anger came tumbling behind it, but she pushed it back. She was going to stay calm if it killed her.

"I guess I'm just too selfish," she said gently.

He nodded. "You did consider it?"

"Of course. I went for counseling about it. I met some wonderful couples looking for babies, people who would have given my boys a great life, probably better than anything I can give them. But in the end…" She shook her head. "I just couldn't do it. I wanted them so much."

He nodded again. "Okay. And you're holding to that decision?"

She stared at him. Just the fact that he could ask a question like that showed how little he understood what parenthood was all about.

"Are you asking me to consider giving them up now? Are you insane?"

He held up a hand. "Okay, okay. I just wanted to make sure. I want to get things perfectly clear between us." He shifted uncomfortably in his seat. "I think we need to establish a base so that we can figure out how we're going to do this. I want to provide for them in an equitable way so that the burden isn't entirely on you."

She stared at him, vaguely aware that he was still talking, going on about monthly payments and trust funds and clothing allowances. He hadn't said a thing about the boys themselves. He wanted to start writing checks to remove himself from the entire mess. He just didn't get it, did he? The anger that had been simmering bubbled up.

"Stop," she said firmly. "I don't want to hear it. It's not money that I need from you."

He looked surprised. "If you're talking about… well, commitments, Darcy, you know I can't…"

She looked away, avoiding his eyes. "I know that. I'm not asking you to completely change your life around."

"So what exactly are you asking from me, Darcy?" he asked softly.

She closed her eyes. It was a darn good question. What she wanted in her heart of hearts was something impossible and she didn't even bother bringing it up. Opening her eyes again, she turned and met his gaze. This was so important. If only she could find the right words to make him understand how very important it really was.

"I've tried to think this through and define what's best for the boys," she said. "They need a dad. You're the first choice. You don't have to marry me to be their dad, you know. If you could imagine just being a presence in their lives…"

Her voice choked and she stopped. He made a move toward her, but she pulled back.

"If you don't think you can do that," she went on in a rush, "I wish you'd tell me right away. Because I'll have to find someone else to be their father-figure."

His blue eyes registered shock at that. "What do you mean?"

She straightened her shoulders, regaining her strength. "I think that was pretty clear. I'll need to marry someone. Someone else," she added hastily.

"Someone else? Who?"

She shook her head, feeling stronger all the time. "Oh, I don't know. There are a few candidates."

"Kevin?" he asked, a hint of scorn in his tone.

She shrugged. "He's a possibility. But actually, I was thinking more along the lines of…" She hesitated, wondering if she really wanted to say this, then rushed ahead. "Bert Lensen in accounting."

"Bert Lensen?" He frowned. "Isn't he that short, chubby, balding guy?"

"Yes. Very nice man. Not married. Seems to like me. Always asks about the twins."

"Uh-huh" He shook his head, looking skeptical. He was beginning to suspect he was being snowed. "I don't know, Darcy. I just don't see you with a man like that."

"No?" Her eyes flashed. "Well, think again. He's perfect, actually."

"Perfect! You're not serious."

"Sure. I'm not looking for a weekend fling," she said pointedly. "I'm looking for a 'slow and steady wins the race' sort of guy. I need a real father for my children. I need someone reliable."

"Unlike me."

She drew breath deep down into her lungs. She could read a deep sense of injury in his gaze. She hadn't meant to hurt him, just make him think a little.

"That's not what I said."

"But it's what you meant." He turned away. "Face it, Darcy. Using your criteria, I'm not good enough to be the father of my own children."

"Mitch! I never said that!"

"You didn't have to say it. It's obvious." He raked his fingers through his hair. "And damn it all," he said gruffly, shifting back to look at her, "you might be right."

She was not going to make a comment. And this had all the signs of a conversation going nowhere. Maybe they needed to take a break from it.

"We ought to get going," she said, staring hard into his blue eyes.

"Sure," he responded, holding her gaze with his own.

Something sizzled in the air between them. The air was suddenly thick and hot and she felt as though she couldn't breathe.

"Why don't you grab those binoculars and let's go take a look at the landscape," she said, reaching for the door handle and making her escape.

He stayed where he was for a moment, watching her get out of the car and walk over to the railing. This was just plain nuts. He'd never felt so out of control. He'd always prided himself on being able to stay detached from the women he had relationships with. He was up-front about what could be expected. No one he'd ever dated had cause to complain—and he'd never stayed in one place or with one woman long enough to build up any sort of commitment expectations.

But everything had gone out of whack with Darcy. From the moment their gazes had met in the rainy doorway, it had been as though something were drawing them together. He'd never felt this way before. And now, when she started talking about marrying Bert Lenson… The first thing he'd felt was an ugly urge to go beat the poor guy to a pulp. The thought of another man touching her was like a knife in his gut. He couldn't stand it. But as of this moment, he had no real claim to her.

Nothing was making any sense.

Swearing softly to himself, he took the binoculars from the glove compartment and left the car to join her at the railing.

CHAPTER SIX

"LOOK," Darcy said, making a wide sweep with her arm. "Texas in the noonday sun. Isn't she beautiful?"

Mitch heard the emotion in her voice and started to smile, but then he looked at what she was presenting to him and he frowned instead. He gazed at the rolling hills, the scattered stands of pecan and live oak, the rocky creek bottoms. A red-tailed hawk was circling a water hole and he thought he caught sight of a white-tailed deer flashing into a thicket.

It suddenly occurred to him that she was right. Why was it he had never noticed before? Texas *was* beautiful.

He'd spent most of the last few years in countries where deep green jungles and jagged mountains and turquoise water defined beautiful landscape. This was a different type of beauty and it resonated deeply with something in his inner core—his heart and soul. Texas was home. It had been a long time since he'd thought of it that way.

He turned and looked at Darcy. She was trying to figure out just where the borders of the Heartland Project stood and she took the binoculars from him to check. He watched the breeze ruffle her hair, exposing her tiny ear. It curled like a pink shell against her head. He wanted to touch it, run a finger around its curve. He moved closer and she looked up from the binoculars, startled to find him so near.

"Uh…I think we can see the border better from that ledge just through those bushes," she said, gesturing toward another vantage point. "I'll go take a look."

She turned and went quickly, as much to flee from the look she'd seen in his eyes as anything else. Her heart was thumping in her chest. She pushed her way through the brush, looking back to see that he was following. And then a branch tangled with her hair.

"Ouch!" She stopped, caught by the bramble, yanking at it and only making matters worse.

"I'll get it," he said, reaching into her hair and prying the tangle loose.

She closed her eyes. He was much too close. She couldn't breathe. He was going to touch her. She knew it without being told.

And there it was. His fingers were still wrapped in her hair, but his lips were on her neck.

"Oh!" she cried, trying without a lot of success to pull away. She swung around to look at him. "Don't."

He held her face in his hands. "Darcy, I can't…"

Can't what? she wondered a bit hysterically, but she knew. He couldn't stop this. Well, neither could she. So who was going to do it?

When his mouth covered hers, she whimpered, as though he were fulfilling a need she'd held back too long, and she opened to him greedily. His hand on her face, his body so close, his mouth on hers. All felt so good, she was afraid she would sink into this ecstasy and never come up for air.

She had to pull away. She had to break this off. She couldn't let this go on for another minute.

Well, maybe just a minute. Or two. For just a little while, could she let herself touch heaven again?

No! She had to be strong. She had to think of her twins.

That did it. She finally pulled away from him, breathless and angry with herself.

"Oh, Mitch!" She wiped her mouth with the back of her hand while staring into his clouded eyes. "Promise me you won't ever do that again."

"I can't," he said very softly, his gaze never leaving hers.

Shaking her head, she tore away from him and hurried back to the car. He caught up with her before she reached it, grabbing her elbow and pulling her around to face him. The moment she looked into his eyes, she was relieved. He looked like a different person.

"You're right, Darcy," he said calmly, dropping

her arm when he could see she wasn't going to run. "Of course you're right. And I'm sorry."

She nodded. "Me, too," she said.

He took a deep breath. "We've got too much emotional baggage between us. We've got to deal with it. We didn't settle things about the twins."

She nodded again. "No, we didn't, did we?"

He grimaced. "We got sidetracked with you talking about marrying Bert Lenson."

She rolled her eyes. "I'm not marrying Bert Lenson."

"Then why did you throw his bald-headed hat into the ring?"

I was only trying to scare you. She couldn't say that out loud, but it was the truth—though she didn't even want to admit it to herself.

"I was just using him as an example of the kind of man my boys need in their lives. I just wanted you to understand the reality of the situation. You should know what's going on."

He shrugged. "You know, I'm a little surprised you even think I should have any say in the matter."

She hesitated. "Look, Mitch. I know you can't be the sort of father I would want for them. But you are their biological father. We have to go from there."

He nodded, searching her eyes. "Just by saying that, you give up a certain amount of control. You understand that, don't you?"

She nodded. "Yes. I know."

He shook his head, studying her as though he could

hardly believe what he saw. "I have to admire your integrity for that. It takes guts to take that sort of risk."

She quickly dampened her dry lips with her tongue. "You know, in a funny way, I trust you. I know you'll do the right thing, whatever we decide that will be."

They stared at each other for a long, long moment.

"Okay," he said, taking her hand to lead her back to the car. "We haven't decided what to do, but we've decided to trust each other. That's a step in the right direction."

She nodded. It really was.

They were back on the road in minutes, pulling out onto the two-lane route, heading back toward the city. Mitch stretched and let out a deep breath. "We need to get something to eat," he said brightly.

"Speak for yourself," she responded tartly.

He looked at her, bemused. "Okay, I will. I could eat a horse."

She almost smiled. "That's a dangerous thing to threaten out here in horse country."

She could see his slow grin out of the edge of her vision. "I'll make do with a burger," he said. He sat up straighter in his seat. "And I know just where we can get one."

"Where?" she asked skeptically. They were out in the middle of nowhere. She hadn't seen a gas station for miles, much less a hamburger stand.

"Turn right on the Sorrel Highway." He pointed out the sign just ahead. "It's been years, but I think it'll still be there."

She turned where he'd indicated, but the land looked empty in that limitless way that didn't bode well for hamburgers. How many miles would he want to go before giving it up as a lost cause?

"It's got to be out this way," he reassured her. "I remember it well. My grandfather had a cattle ranch in the Sargosa Hills and I used to go out and help him work the place sometimes on summer vacations. There was this old recluse of a guy—think of your ultimate stereotype of the old prospector with a pickax on his shoulder and a mule by his side. His name was Ry Tanner."

He scanned the horizon, then pointed as a ramshackle building came into view. "There it is! See that bed and breakfast? That's got to be the place. Stop there."

Darcy frowned doubtfully as they pulled up in front of the ancient building. A two-story frame in a rustic Victorian style, standing out alone on the treeless plain, it looked like a survivor of another age. The sign said, Tree Stump Bed And Breakfast. Another sign, hanging by a tattered rope, said, Café. And there were a few tables and chairs set out on the browning grass of the front yard, in the shade of a small stand of cottonwood trees.

"Mitch, are you sure?" she began.

"Absolutely," he said, getting out of the car. "We can get some lunch here. Come on."

She followed him but she wasn't too keen on this. The place almost looked abandoned.

"I don't know," she murmured, frowning.

But Mitch was cupping his hands and calling toward the entry to the building. "Hello! Anybody here?"

There was a dusty silence for a moment, but just as Darcy was starting to turn away, a gruff voice came from the house.

"Go away. We're closed."

Mitch grinned, giving Darcy a wink. "It's him," he said before stepping closer. "Ry Tanner, ya ole reprobate. Is that you?"

There was a pause, then the voice sounded again. "We're closed, I tell you."

But Mitch had mounted the steps to the front door and was peering in through the milky glass. "Ry Tanner, come on out here."

"Who's that?" the voice demanded.

"Mitch Carver." He spread out his arms. "Don't you remember me?"

The door opened a crack and a grizzled head appeared. "Mitch Carver! Is that you?"

"It's me, all right."

The door opened a bit more and the old man stood in the light. "What are you doin' here? I ain't seen you for years." His gnarled face turned and his beady black eyes took in Darcy, too. "And you got yourself a pretty girl. Poor thing. I never thought you'd find one would put up with ya."

Mitch laughed. "She doesn't. But that's another story."

The man shuffled out onto the porch and nodded toward the tables on the grass. "Come on over and set a spell," he said. "Out here in the cool breeze."

"We came to get some food," Mitch said as they followed him to the table.

He shook his gray head. "We're closed."

"A little snack will do. That's all we need."

Dropping down into a chair, Ry Tanner frowned at his company. "I told you, we're closed."

"No, we ain't." A plump, pretty woman who looked to be in her forties came out of the house. "Don't listen to him," she said, smiling at them all. "He's just playin' hermit. You're old friends of his? Y'all sit down. I'll get you some food."

Ry grumbled, but it was becoming apparent that his grumbling didn't mean much. Darcy and Mitch sat down across from him and the woman, whose name was Betty, took their order and hurried into the house to prepare their food.

"You two married yet?" Ry demanded, glaring at Darcy.

"No!" they both said at once.

He nodded, looking at Mitch. "Good." He leaned closer, confiding. "But you watch out. Here's a life lesson, son. They try to trap you."

"Trap?" Darcy knew he was just an old man but she couldn't hide her outrage. "Why would I want to trap anyone?"

He glanced at her, then back at Mitch. "Marriage. That's all any woman wants, you know. She wants to pluck you off the vine and plunk you down into her own little teacup."

Darcy blinked at the strangely mixed metaphor.

"I have never tried to trap anyone into anything, much less marriage. And you know what? I'll tell you a secret." She leaned toward him conspiratorially. "I wouldn't marry him if he asked me to."

"See?" He waved a finger in the air. "That's the first trick they use. Playin' hard to get." He nodded knowingly, narrowing his eyes as he looked at her sideways. "Watch out for that one, my friend."

She shook her head. Mitch was silently laughing, his blue eyes dancing. She glared at him. He was having too much fun with this.

"The male ego never ceases to amaze me," she muttered.

Ry seemed to take offense. "Well then, what are you coming by here bothering people fer?"

Darcy's jaw dropped. This crazy old man! "We don't mean to bother you. Mitch just thought…"

He looked triumphant. "Ya see there?" He nodded to Mitch. "There she goes, takin' your side, letting you think she's defending you. That's number two on the roster. Write these down, son. You need to keep a list about you at all times. Ya gotta be prepared to counter their attacks."

Mitch was laughing, Darcy was confused between reluctant amusement and annoyance, and Ry Tanner seemed to be in his element now.

But Betty had her own advice. "Don't listen to him," she suggested as she put a pair of huge hamburgers, with fries, out in front of them. "He just likes to hear himself talk. Don't you, Pops?"

Ry grumbled, but the hamburgers were good and Darcy was famished. She had to admit the old man was like a piece of old Texas. He should be in a museum somewhere. But she couldn't say he was much of a lunch companion. Mitch seemed to have a strange affection for this old man, but she didn't think she could share it.

"So, Ry Tanner," Mitch was saying casually. "What do you know about the Heartland Project? I hear it's going in right next to you here, isn't it?"

Ry nodded. "Yes, that's true. They even wanted to buy out my land. But I'm hangin' tough." He shook his head. "We'll see."

Darcy's eyes widened and she stared at Mitch. The two men went on talking about the project, about what was being planned and how Ry's land might enter into the deal, but she hardly listened. So this was what Mitch had come along with her for, this was what had been his reason for hunting down Ry Tanner.

And here, a part of her had been thinking he might

just have wanted to be with her. And that part of her had been reveling in that hope, hadn't it?

What a fool she was! In the first place, for wanting him to want to be with her. And in the second place, for wanting that despite the danger it posed. Was she crazy? So it seemed. That did it. She was going to have to be much tougher on herself from now on. After all, she'd fallen for this man's charm before. She had a record to live down. She had to be doubly careful.

Mitch had a devilish look in his eyes as they walked back to the car. She glanced at him suspiciously. "What?" she asked him.

He leaned against the car door and his gaze rose slowly to meet hers. "The Heartland Project," he said softly. "I want it."

She stared at him, mouth agape. "You're crazy!"

"Pipe down," he warned, laughing at her. "Get in the car. Let's not advertise it."

"There is no way you can get that project," she went on as she slipped into the driver's seat. "You know that, don't you? There are plenty of big boys after it. Ned Varner, for one."

"Ned Varner has been my family's nemesis for years, you know," he told her casually. "He makes moves every time he thinks my father's hold on the company is weak. Fear of what he was up to was the very reason my mother got me to come home."

"Oh. Well, I'm sure she was thinking defensively,

not for you to try a suicidal move like trying for the Heartland Project."

His head rose and he had a steely look. "I'm going after it."

She was astonished at his crazy naive attitude. "What are you talking about? You don't have the experience, the background. You don't know what you're doing!"

"I could do it." His blue eyes were intense as they held hers. "You and me together. You can teach me the ropes. I'm a quick study."

Her breath caught in her throat. "Wait a minute. Why would I be teaching you the ropes?" She threw her hands up. "If I know so much, why aren't I heading the project?"

"Because you don't have the credentials." Reaching out, he cupped her cheek in his hand and looked deeply into her eyes. "Let's face it, Darcy. They won't let you. But you and me together—we could do it."

His touch was something between fire and silk, and she knew it could act on her like a drug. She pulled away, shaking her head. "You're nuts," she said, starting the car.

She was fuming and he was making jokes. He wanted the Heartland Project, and he wanted to use her to help get it. Now wasn't that just special! If she wasn't careful she would get roped into having even more of her life taken over by this man. Who did he think he was, anyway?

But she knew the answer to that, didn't she? Oh! She wanted to scream.

Still, she managed to control herself and she was quiet most of the way back into town. So was Mitch.

Probably thinking over ways to get her to pull in the Heartland Project for him. That was not going to happen!

But how was she going to avoid it, working for him in that office every day? She'd known this was going to be a problem from the beginning.

"It's Friday night," he said suddenly, as they entered the city limits. "Date night. Have you got a date?"

"Yes, as a matter of fact, I do," she said, tossing her hair back and looking at him sideways.

"Oh." That surprised him. "So who's the lucky guy? Bert Lenson?"

Was that sarcasm she heard? Had to be.

"There are two of them, actually," she told him. "A couple of very special guys. We're planning to paint the town. If things really get hot, I might even let them stay up past their bedtime."

He'd realized what she was doing long before she wrapped it up and he waited, a twisted smile on his face. "The joys of motherhood," he said dryly.

That put her back up but she held back the sharp comment that came to mind. "I suppose you've got plenty of old girlfriends you could look up," she said instead.

He laughed. "Oh sure. There are old girlfriends of

mine scattered all over the San Antonio area. Terra Dulce is crawling with them."

"I would have thought so."

He turned in his seat, shaking his head. "Are you crazy? Look how old I am, Darcy. All my old girl-friends are too busy organizing car pools for their kids to give me the time of day. Arguably some of them will be divorced, but still…"

"Ah, it's the kids that turn you off, is it?"

"I didn't say that."

She pulled onto the local freeway. They were almost back at work. "What do you have against kids?"

"I don't have anything against them," he said, though he sounded a bit too defensive. "I've dealt with kids before. Last year I hid out with a woman who had two kids and I spent a lot of time helping her take care of them. I can give bottles. I can even change a diaper if I have to. I don't want to. But I can. I'm not totally clueless."

But Darcy was still hung up on what he'd said at that beginning of that monologue. "'Hid out'?"

He sighed, hesitated, then shook his head. "It's a long story. Forget it for now. Someday I'll tell you all about it."

She could tell by the finality in his voice that these were his last words on the subject—for now, at least. She turned into the ACW parking lot and pulled into her space.

"Well, that was fun," she murmured, turning off

the engine and starting to gather her things to get out of the car. And then she noticed he was still sitting there, making no move to exit. He had the look on his face that she was beginning to realize meant he had something he wanted to say. So she settled back into her seat and sighed.

"Okay. Out with it."

"Darcy, I've been thinking."

Here it came. He had big plans for things she could do to help him win that darn project.

"Yes?" she said.

He was quiet for a moment, then turned and looked into her face.

"Okay, here's the deal. I think we should get married."

"What?" She couldn't have been more surprised.

"I was thinking that maybe we should reconsider this marriage thing."

She was struggling for breath.

"Why?"

"If you look at it objectively, it's only fair. This whole situation is as much my fault as it is yours."

The man had experienced an epiphany. "Oh, you think so?"

He was frowning thoughtfully. "I realize I've taken too long to come to this decision, but you've got to admit, the twins threw me way off kilter. You had nine months to get used to the idea of having kids before they even got here. I didn't get that luxury."

"But Mitch…"

"It won't be a normal marriage," he added quickly. "I'll be gone most of the time. But at least we'll be married."

She stared at him. This was one spectacular turn-around—only a few hours ago he'd been staunchly declaring he would never marry. Or had she heard that wrong? Whatever it was, she didn't think she had better rely on it. Besides, he still hadn't mentioned the babies.

"Let me get this straight. We'll be married, but you'll be gone most of the time."

He nodded, his eyes bright with confidence. "That's about the size of it."

"I see." She gave him a wry smile. "So you want to tie me down while you are free to go off and do whatever strikes your fancy."

His look darkened a little. "Well, kind of. Though that isn't exactly the way I was thinking of it. You're putting it a bit unfairly."

She looked at him and laughed. She knew that a part of her would always be bound to him no matter what they did. But she had to stay hardened against him. He still hadn't made one gesture toward the boys. If he didn't feel anything for the twins, the rest of this was moot. She didn't even want him in her life.

"Darcy, think about it," he was saying, trying to be convincing. "It could work. There would be advantages. I could check in periodically, sort of like military guys do. If you could live with a part-time husband…"

"No."

"No?" He looked surprised.

Her steady gaze pinned him back. "It sounds like a great idea—for you. You'd be having your cake and eating it, too."

He thought about it for a moment, then shrugged. "What's wrong with that?"

"Mitch…"

"Okay, I'll put it this way." He grabbed her hand and brought it to his lips, then gazed at her over it. "Darcy, will you marry me?"

Something very like a butterfly was flapping around in her stomach. She was very close to being sick. This was so like what she'd dreamed of, and yet, it wasn't good enough. She pulled her hand away from him.

"I can't marry you."

"Why not?"

"You are not marriage material. We knew that from the beginning. Nothing's changed."

He stared at her, his blue eyes turned black as night in the dim light of the parking structure. "That's where you're wrong, Darcy. No matter what we decide here, everything's changed."

CHAPTER SEVEN

"YOU know," Darcy mused to herself in the mirror two days later. "Just when you least expect it, fate will step in and take control. Happens every time."

She'd been going crazy wondering what she was going to do about Mitch. She was half in love with the man and there were reasons for her to want him in her life. And yet, she knew very well that would lead to nothing but heartbreak in the long run. So it was just too dangerous being around him all the time. If she wasn't careful, he was going to lure her back into his influence and she was going to find herself agreeing to one of his loony ideas—like getting married. And that would be disastrous.

But now, like manna from the heavens, came a reprieve. That very morning, Mimi had announced that she had to go out of town.

"I'm so sorry to do this to you, Darcy. And at such a time. But my sister has fallen and wrenched her back. They might have to operate. She has no family to take care of her, and no money for nursing care, so I have to go."

"Of course you must go," Darcy told her, silently sending up a cheer as she realized the implications. "How long do you think you'll be?"

"Oh, two weeks at least."

"Oh, good."

"What?" Mimi looked puzzled.

Darcy gave her a dazzling smile and amended quickly. "I mean, you're so good—to your sister. She's lucky she has you."

"Well, I hate to leave you in the lurch. I'm going to call around to everyone I know and see if I can find someone to watch the babies."

"No, you're not," Darcy told her sweetly. "I'm going to watch them. I'll take some time off. I'll just have to stay home for a couple of weeks. It'll be perfect."

"Oh, but doesn't Mitch need you?"

Mitch can go pound sand! she thought, with vengeance on her mind. A couple of weeks away from Mitch—nothing could be better at a time like this. This would reaffirm her bond with her children plus she would get away from Mitch's influence. With a little bit of distance, maybe she could think things through more clearly. It was all good.

But aloud, she said, "He'll be fine. There are plenty of women at ACW who would be happy to take my place, believe me."

She went in to work Monday morning with a spring in her step. She stopped by Human Resources to deal with the paperwork, then breezed into the office almost an hour after the workday had begun. Mitch scowled at her as she stood before him at his desk.

"Where have you been?"

Her bright smile was genuine. "Good morning to you, too."

His grouchy mood melted immediately. "Yeah, well… Hey, I missed you," he said lightly. "It was a long weekend."

Her smile grew a little more forced. He looked very appealing in the morning sunlight that streamed in from the huge windows, especially now that the look in his eyes had warmed. Just looking at him made her heart beat a little faster—which was exactly why she had to go.

"Well, I'm afraid that's something you're going to have to get used to," she said. "I'm not going to be here for a while."

His scowl was back and he rose from his chair. "What are you talking about?"

"I need to take a few days off."

His frown deepened. "Why?"

She wasn't really fond of his tone, so she developed a frown of her own. "I have some personal days coming," she said defensively. "I'm going to take them."

He looked angered and frustrated at the same time. "Why are you taking them now?"

She glared at him. "Do you have to know everything I do?"

"Yes." He hesitated, as though he rather regretted having said that. "After all, you're taking care of my children," he improvised.

"Oh, for heaven's sake." She gaped at him. The nerve of the man! He had the decency to look chagrined—but only for a moment before his natural arrogance reasserted itself.

"Okay," she said quickly. "This is what's happening. Mimi has to go take care of her sister in Dallas, so I'm going to have to stay home with the twins until she gets back."

He shook his head as though he couldn't see what that had to do with anything. "Can't you hire a sitter?"

"Mitch, these are babies. *My* babies. I would hire a stranger if I absolutely had to, but I don't have to. I have the time accrued. And I'm going to take it."

Frowning again, he rubbed a hand through his hair, making it stand up at crazy angles. "But you can't go now. We're wrapping up the Bermuda Woods job. That was your baby before I got here."

She threw out her hands. "You know very well that is basically signed and sealed and only needs to be delivered. Skylar Mars can handle any loose ends."

"Skylar?"

"I talked to HR and set it up. She's taking my

place. You know who she is. She was one of the ladies who had a morning party for you the other day. The redhead."

"Ah." His eyes lit up as he remembered her. And who could blame him? She was quite a beauty. But Darcy had to admit, that look on his face rankled. Still, it didn't last long. Very quickly he was frowning again.

"Well, she may be decorative and know how to present a plan, but does she have any experience with anything like the Heartland Project?"

Darcy hesitated. That was a sore spot. "She can call me for advice any time," she said. "I won't be going anywhere. Except the park." Come to think of it, she did have a few things planned. She began to count them off on her fingers. "And the market. And the doctor's on Wednesday. And the boys' playdate on Thursday. And…"

"Phone calls aren't the same as having first class expertise sitting right here in the office," he interjected impatiently.

Darcy knew that, but Skylar was about as good as he was going to get. "She's done property before," she reassured him. "She'll do everything you need."

He thought that over seriously, but when he met her gaze again he looked a little lost. "But you're what I need," he said, as though it surprised him, too.

Her heart gave a little jog, but she looked at him hard, sure he didn't mean that the way it sounded.

"Sorry," she said quickly. "I've got two weeks coming to me and I'm going to take them."

His face hardened and his tone did, too. Pleading wasn't working. He looked like he'd decided to resort to strong-arm tactics. "You can't. Not now."

She straightened her shoulders. "Yes, I can."

"I'm your boss, Darcy. And I say you can't."

"I've been working here longer than you and have more street clout," she asserted, knowing what she was saying was ridiculous. "More pull with the people who make this company work."

"Oh, yeah?"

"Yeah!"

He glared at her. "I'll have you fired."

Her chin was out a mile. "Great. You do that. That will solve all my problems."

Well, not really. But it would solve one. The big one. The one she was merely avoiding by staying away from him for two weeks. But it was a step in the right direction. Maybe with time, the problem would find its own solution. On the other hand, maybe she was just kicking the can down the road. Either way, she would have two weeks away from this emotional cauldron.

She looked at him, so tall and hard and handsome, and something very much like a lump rose in her throat. He stood silhouetted before his big picture window, looking like a big tycoon. He was the boss and he looked the part. No more romantic renegade. He was a man of corporate power now.

But he wasn't going to fire her and she knew it. She turned to go. He blocked her way, taking hold of her upper arms and staring down into her face.

"Please don't do this, Darcy," he said, his voice soft but hiding a core of steel. "I need you here."

She looked up into his eyes and began to melt. Those gorgeous blue eyes, those thick dark lashes, that flash of excitement—she could hardly breathe. Everything in her yearned toward him. Closing her eyes, she thought of her babies and gathered strength.

"I have to go," she told him, pulling away. "See you in two weeks."

She walked quickly toward the elevator, sure that he would follow her, take her into his arms, make her stay. That scared her. But when it didn't happen, there was suddenly a big empty hole in her sense of well-being. It should have been a relief, but instead, she wanted to cry.

Mitch was in a very bad mood. Office life without Darcy was a whole different animal—an animal he wasn't very fond of. Skylar was definitely beautiful. Very easy on the eyes. Oh, yes. But there was one problem. Skylar never shut up.

It wasn't so much that she talked to Mitch all the time. He could handle that. A couple of sharp comments and a raised eyebrow had pretty much nipped most of that in the bud. But she talked to everyone else—incessantly. Everyone who walked by her desk, everyone who emerged from the elevator, everyone who called on the phone, got at least a ten-minute conversation. Even when he shut the door to his inner office, her laughter penetrated. That sound could probably bend steel. It certainly raised the hair on the back of his neck, and not in a good way. It also set his teeth on edge. And most of all, it made him think longingly of Darcy.

It had been a long time since he'd worked in an office environment and he hadn't realized how much Darcy had helped transition him back into the groove until she wasn't there to help him anymore. He needed her here.

He needed her here for purely selfish reasons, but that wasn't all. He'd thought that they would talk more about his idea. He'd had this feeling from the first that marriage was the only way to solve their problems, and he'd resisted because it went against everything he'd planned for his life. But the more he'd thought about it, the more he'd realized it might be an answer for them both.

He'd seen men out in the field who had cracked up over time. The work he did out there was stressful, to say the least. It wouldn't hurt to have an anchor at home, something to help keep him on an even keel. He'd never known a woman he could even remotely imagine marrying. But Darcy—well, she was different. Maybe…maybe it would work with her.

He hadn't taken her vehement rejection of his idea

too seriously. She hadn't had time to think it over yet. If she were here, they could talk it over and find a way to make it work. If she wasn't here, they couldn't do a thing about it. He needed her here.

That laugh again. He shuddered. Turning to his computer screen, he did a search on "Noise canceling headphones." Hmm. It was a possibility.

"Mitch?"

Skylar came in, looking coy. "I hate to bother you, but the manager out at Bermuda Woods just called and he says there's a document missing from the final packet."

Mitch shrugged. "So find it and get it out to him," he said dismissively.

She hesitated, then smiled flirtatiously. "He told me a bunch of stuff but I can't figure out what he's talking about. I thought maybe we could work on it together. I could really use your help." She looked hopeful.

Mitch frowned. "I'm not up to speed on that project, either." He sighed resignedly. "Okay, we'd better call her."

Skylar blinked. "Call who?"

"Darcy Connors, of course. She knows everything about this stuff."

"Oh." Skylar didn't look enthusiastic.

"Dial her up." He waved her toward the phone. "Let's get her input."

Skylar sighed big. "Okay."

She looked up Darcy's number and pushed the numbers on the phone.

"Oh darn, it's her machine," she told Mitch, waving the receiver in the air.

"Well, leave a message," he said impatiently.

"Oh. Okay." She put the receiver to her ear. "Hi, Darcy, honey. It's Skylar—at the office? Mr. Carver—Mitch—he would like to talk to you about—um—the Bermuda Woods development. He has some loose ends he wants to discuss. Please call us back. Okay? Thanks. See you soon, honey."

Mitch scowled and glanced at his watch. "If she doesn't call in half an hour, call her again," he ordered gruffly.

Skylar tossed back her fire-engine-red hair, looked like she was going to launch into a diatribe, then stopped herself when she caught the expression on his face. "Whatever," she said, rolling her eyes and flouncing out of the office.

Mitch's teeth were on edge again.

"Whatever," he echoed dully, staring out his window at the growing storm clouds. "Whatever it takes," he added more softly, his gaze sharpening. He needed a plan. He was a man of action, wasn't he? All right then. He would come up with a plan. How hard could that be?

Darcy sat in Mimi's kitchen listening to the message as Skylar gave it. There was no way she was picking up the phone to take the call. She was going to stay strong, even though she knew Mitch was right there, just seconds away. She'd promised she would take calls and help when needed. And she planned to be available by the end of the week. But not now. It was too soon. She and Mitch both needed to get used to the reality of her not being in the office. She couldn't think of anything that couldn't wait a few days. So she was standing pat.

She hadn't realized it would be this hard. She'd managed to remove Mitch from her daily life physically, but there didn't seem to be any way to push him out of her mind.

Still, she was having fun with the twins. Tonight she was making pizza and had games and songs ready. Tomorrow she was taking them to the park. If only she wasn't haunted every step by thoughts of how much Mitch would like these little guys—if he ever let himself.

That night it rained hard for a while. A little thunder. A little lightning. After checking on her babies who were sleeping through the turmoil, Darcy snuggled under her covers and listened to the storm. Was Mitch awake, too? Was he lying there, just a few miles away, staring at the ceiling of his room and thinking of her? For just a moment she could imagine reaching out and making a magical connection. She shivered delightfully, then closed her eyes and dreamed of him.

The next day she ignored another phone message from Skylar—the third one, and packed the boys into the car, taking off for the park. They had a wonderful, if tiring couple of hours, stopped for ice-cream cones on the way home, which turned the inside of her car into a sticky zone, then headed for home.

She knew something was wrong right away. For one thing, Mitch's car was standing out in front of her house. But even more ominous, a moving truck was coming out of her driveway and taking off just as she drove up. She looked back. The two boys were sound asleep in their car seats. She debated leaving them there for a few minutes, then decided against it. You just couldn't be too careful where these young lives were concerned.

That meant she had to take time lugging both car seats into the house. The boys didn't wake up, so at least she got a break there. She left them on the floor of their room with their seats tilted back into sleeping position, and hurried back into the living room to see what the heck was going on.

She could see his car still parked at the curb, but there was no sign of him outside. So that meant he was probably inside somewhere, but where? The garage was her next target, but it was standing empty. She frowned. Maybe the converted sunporch on the side of the house. She hurried to it and opened the wide French doors that led onto the porch. And there he was.

"Hi," he said, leaning back in his desk chair. "I've been waiting for you. Where've you been?"

She gaped at him in consternation, then went down the three steps to his level. He was looking like the cat that ate the canary, very bright-eyed and full of himself, and he was surrounded by an instant office that he must have set up in the short space of time she'd spent out with the boys.

"What in the world…?" she muttered, in shock as she looked at the sparkling glass desk, equipped with a trendy slender notebook computer, printer, fax and copy machine—even his trademark big jar of jelly beans. A huge metal file cabinet sat beside the desk. All the comforts of the office gleaming attractively.

"How did you get in here?" she demanded.

He raised one eyebrow. "Please, Darcy. It's a basic requirement of my profession to know how to get into locked places."

Of course. She knew that. But…but… he wasn't supposed to get into *her* locked places!

"You couldn't wait until I got home?"

"No. The moving van was on a tight schedule."

"Moving van…" She could hardly talk. In her wildest dreams she had never expected this. "But why?"

"Would you believe that my parents kicked me out? Just like high school."

She shook her head, unable to compute what he'd

just said. "Kicked you out of what? It's the middle of the day."

He shrugged. "I was only kidding. Actually I left voluntarily. I couldn't take another day in that house."

It was only then that she noticed a large cot had been added to the wicker decor of the room. She stared at it for a moment, taking in the big fluffy comforter and the pillow with teddy bears parading across its case. She turned back to look at him. He hadn't just moved in his work-a-day operation, he'd moved in his entire life.

"You've completely moved in?" she cried, reeling from the implications.

He nodded casually, as though this were nothing outrageous. "I had to go somewhere."

She glared at him and waved one arm in the air. "Then set up a bed at the office. Your *real* office."

He shook his head firmly, as though she just didn't understand the circumstances and would agree if only she did. "I also couldn't stand another day at that office. Not while Skylar walks those echoing marble halls."

She blinked, confused. "Skylar? What's wrong with Skylar?"

He grimaced painfully. "Have you ever tried to work with her? If you had, you wouldn't need to ask."

"She…she…" Somehow she couldn't go any further than that one word.

But he took up the slack without missing a beat. "I was in a quandary. I couldn't work, I couldn't think, I couldn't sleep. So I decided the best plan of action was a direct trek to your house. I brought all the stuff I need to work. And I figure I'll camp out here for the duration."

"No." She was shaking her head. This was impossible. *He* was impossible. Life, at the moment, was impossible. "Oh, no, you won't."

He sighed as though her lack of a charitable response pained him deeply. "I won't be in your hair constantly. I promise. I'll be over here, out of the way. But when I need you for something, I can call you over and—"

"This is just typical of you, isn't it?" she demanded with fury, leaning toward him across the desk. "You see everything through the same prism— what would be best for *you*. Did it ever occur to you that I might have other priorities right now?"

He looked puzzled. "No, actually. I thought maybe you'd be glad for the company. Time can really drag when you're required to talk nothing but baby gibberish all day."

"How would you know?"

He half laughed. "Darcy, I keep trying to make you understand that I've got a broad experience with the ways of the world. I know a lot. About everything."

"Even children."

"Well, probably not as much as you."

"Oh my goodness, what an admission," she said sarcastically. "Well, you're guaranteed to learn a lot more about children than you've ever wanted to know if you think you're staying here," she warned.

He actually looked surprised. "Not if you keep them in their play area. This is a work area."

She stared at him. Was he for real? "I'm warning you, Mitch. The kids will not be kept out of your way. The kids are center stage in this house. If you want a pure work environment, go back to work."

He took a deep breath and obviously decided not to say what first came trippingly to his tongue. "It's good that we're discussing this," he said unconvincingly. "This way we can work to establish the parameters of our working relationship."

She couldn't believe he could be such a dunderhead. "Mitch, get a clue! There's no working relationship. I'm here mothering and you're intruding."

"Darcy, calm down. This is all for the best, believe me."

That did it. She'd never been so furious. Reaching out she grabbed his newly installed phone and began punching buttons.

"What are you doing?" he asked pleasantly, still leaning back in the desk chair as though all was well with his world and her anger was just a minor passing squall.

She glared at him. "I'm calling the police. I've got an intruder in the house."

"Oh. Good idea." He smiled at her. "Did I get a

chance to tell you my cousin Daniel just made captain of the Terra Dulce Police Force? Oh, and Justin Cabrera, my best friend from kindergarten is on the day desk these days. You'll probably talk to him first. Tell him 'hi' for me, okay?"

She stared at him for a moment as she digested this news, then slammed down the phone. "What— does your family own this town?"

He grinned. "Let's just say the Carvers have impact in Terra Dulce. Always have. Funny, I hated that when I was growing up. Now I'm finding it can come in quite handy."

She wanted to wring his neck. She looked at it, imagining her fingers there, slowly tightening. But that proved self-defeating. Touching his neck would quickly turn into something sensual. There was just no escaping the fact that the man turned her on.

"You're impossible."

"That's probably true." His face softened. "Aw, come on, Darcy. Grin and bear it. It won't be so bad." He waited a moment and when he didn't see any relenting on her part, he sighed. "Okay, I should have called first. I should have warned you what I was planning. But you would have marshaled your forces against me, wouldn't you?"

She gave him the barest of assenting nods.

"I have no idea how many muscular bruiser guys you could have invited over to take a whack at me. I didn't think it was worth risking, when I'm so sure you're going to be glad I move in when all is said and done."

"Really?"

"You wait and see." He tried to coax a smile from her. "I had to do this. I wasn't getting anything done without you. And if I'd been locked up with Skylar much longer, I would probably have to start pricing cement shoes."

The thought almost made her smile, but she managed to control it. "For her or for you?" she asked.

He grinned and she could see that he thought she was weakening. And darn it all—he was probably right. After all, he was so…installed. She didn't have a clue how she could pry him loose. And she heard the boys beginning to stir.

And, truth to tell, there was a little place down deep in her heart that was glad he was here. That just showed that she was losing it.

"Just for one night," she warned him as she left to take care of her babies.

"We'll see," he said, cocky as ever. "Maybe having me around will grow on you."

"Yeah, right," she said dryly. But she was already out of earshot by then. And she had a silly smile on her face. This was just plain hopeless.

CHAPTER EIGHT

THE funny thing was, despite everything, Mitch was getting more work done here than he had at the office. He could hear Darcy in the other room, talking to her babies, doing housework, playing a CD and singing in that great bluesy voice for the children. It was... sort of nice. Something about being this close to Darcy seemed to put his mind at rest in a strange way.

But maybe he was making too much of it. Probably it was just that he no longer had to waste time wondering how he was going to get her back at work. Now he'd taken work to her. So that problem was solved.

He worked through the afternoon. Darcy stopped by while the babies were down for a nap. He looked up to see her standing behind the French doors and he motioned for her to come on in.

"How's it coming?" she asked him. She looked a bit edgy, as though she couldn't get used to his being here in her house. That seemed so different from the reaction he was having, he had to smile, but it did make him a little sad. If only she could accept his good intentions, things would go more smoothly.

"Great. I'm going gangbusters here. But I could use a little feedback from you."

She hesitated. "All right," she conceded, dropping into a chair across the desk from him. He got her to help composing a letter, then made her run through some options on a real estate campaign he'd been asked to give some input on. She responded willingly enough, then looked at all his equipment in wonder.

"How *did* you get all this stuff in here so quickly?" she asked him.

He smiled. "I hire good people. That's why I need you."

She made a face at him. "Too much flattery and I'll stop believing it," she warned.

He laughed. "That's what I like about you, Darcy. You're about the most honest person I know."

A small smile trembled on her lips. "So I've got you fooled, at least," she murmured.

He grinned, leaning forward. "Listen, I want to get started on the Heartland submission. You know the right people. You know what has to be done to win the competition for the job. I'd like you to start working up an outline of our game plan."

Her gaze was hooded and it was a moment before she answered him. "What makes you so sure I want you to win?" she asked.

That set him back on his heels. It had never occurred to him that she wouldn't be in his corner. He frowned, studying her face.

"Why wouldn't you want me to win?"

She licked her lips. "This development is going to take years. You don't plan to be here that long."

He nodded slowly. She had him there. "You're right. I don't."

A spark of something that looked very much like outrage flashed in her eyes. "Then why on earth are you so intent on winning it?"

He drew in a deep breath. He couldn't tell her that. He couldn't even articulate his reasons in words to himself. He knew the feelings involved. Oh brother, did he ever know them. But that wasn't something he could communicate to her. He wouldn't know where to begin.

He knew it had something to do with proving himself to his father. And it had a lot to do with wanting to make sure Ned Varner didn't get the contract. But there was more there. Maybe someday he'd be able to articulate it.

"My reasons don't matter," he said at last, trying to sound crisp and logical. "What I want to do is prove I can do it if I put my mind to it."

"And then you'll walk off and leave the rest of us to pick up the pieces?"

"No." He frowned, realizing she was dealing with much more than what she was actually expressing in words. There was too much emotion in her voice for this just to be about the Heartland Project. "I'll set up a team and give it a vision. I would never abandon a project like that. The groundwork will be laid. I'll do it right."

There were bright red spots on her cheeks. She rose stiffly. "Talk to me again when you're serious," she said.

"I'm very serious," he responded. But she walked away.

He frowned, somewhat baffled by her behavior. She was upset and he wasn't completely sure why. Oh, he had some idea that it had something to do with him and her lack of faith in his staying power. But that fear wasn't based on anything real. She would see that soon, and her misgivings would pass. He really did need her for this project.

Pushing that concern away, he went back to work on some other things he'd been assigned, and a few items he'd taken up on his own. After all, if he was to make an impression in this job, he had to go way beyond the bottom line expectations. Way beyond. Otherwise, what was he here for?

An hour later he was agonizing over a flow chart when he felt something. The hair prickled on the back of his neck. He definitely had the sense of being watched. Maybe Darcy had undergone a change of heart and was hesitating just outside the room.

Turning quickly, he looked up at the wide French

doors, expecting to see her there. Instead he found two sets of blue eyes gazing down at him, plus the dark brown eyes of the dog.

"Hi guys," he said, waving at them.

The only one who responded was the dog, who wagged his tail enthusiastically. The boys didn't move a muscle. He stopped waving. Par for the course. Dogs always did like him. He seemed to be striking out with little boys however.

Suddenly Darcy appeared. He stopped dead and stared at her. She was wearing tight blue jeans and a black V-neck shirt that plunged to reveal a lot of nice cleavage. Her hair was loose and flying about her face. She looked deliciously sexy. Staring at her, he felt an odd quivering inside. As though she'd read his mind, she threw him a glance so piercing, it might have turned a lesser man to stone. Then she herded the boys and dog away from the window. He watched for a few more minutes, but only the dog came back.

Suddenly he felt a little lonely. It was almost time to call it a day. He contemplated throwing in the towel for now and going in to the main house to join them, but then he remembered that he hadn't been invited to do that. It might be prudent to wait until he was asked. So he got back to work. He had to do something to pass the time, after all.

Half an hour later he looked up and the boys were at the door again. That made him smile, even though their faces were still stuck on deadpan. They were obviously checking him out. And good for them. He had to admit, they were a pair of darn fine-looking kids—even if he did say so himself.

"Good genes," he muttered to himself proudly. He waved at them. They stared. He sighed.

"Where's the dog?" he called to them.

But they didn't answer. And when he looked up again, they were gone.

It was almost an hour later when Darcy came to ask him if he would like to join her for something to eat.

"I've put the boys to bed," she told him. "So they won't bother you."

"They don't bother me." He gazed at her steadily. "Darcy, I like kids. Don't pretend I'm a monster."

She finally smiled. "Good," she said. "Now come on before the stroganoff gets cold."

He loved stroganoff. She'd set places at the kitchen table. Red napkins. Blue plates. He was gratified when she brought out a bottle of white wine and poured two glasses. At least she was going to let this seem like a real meal and not a grudge feeding of necessity. She was still wearing the tight pants and the low-cut shirt and he was feeling definitely warm and toasty all around. He raised his glass.

"To women who brighten our lives," he said.

"To men who bully and manipulate," she countered, clinking before he had a chance to draw away.

"That was sneaky," he protested, but he didn't

pursue it. Things seemed to be going well right now. No reason to rock the boat.

The food was great, from the creamy stroganoff on pasta to the leafy green salad and the cherry cobbler for dessert. They chatted inconsequentially, falling back into the pattern of banter threaded through more serious conversation they had developed in Paris. By the end of the meal, Darcy was laughing and looking as relaxed and happy as he'd ever seen her. And he was burning to take her in his arms.

But he couldn't do that. Not only would it complicate matters, it would probably result in her kicking him out on his ear, and he didn't relish sleeping in his car tonight.

He stayed in the kitchen and helped her with the dishes and they talked about ACW, and then about what he'd been doing all these years, staying so far away from Texas.

"Tell me about your work overseas these last few years," she said, handing him a stack of plates to put away in an upper cabinet.

"What about it?" He reached high and confidently slid the plates into place for her.

She leaned against the counter, watching him. "What is it that draws you so strongly to it? How did you get this way?"

He put away his drying towel, then leaned against the counter facing her. "You know that I joined the Army after my freshman year of college," he said.

She frowned. "I thought you had a degree."

"I got that later with the Army's help," he said. "I was in Special Forces for eight years. By then I was ready for a change, so I got out and joined a firm that does security work all over the world."

She nodded. "Okay, I knew that. My impression is that you were doing pretty much the same thing you'd done in the Army, only getting paid better."

He grinned. "That was just about it."

"So would you call what you do being a mercenary?" she asked tentatively, as though she was afraid he might take offense at the term. And in truth, he did.

"A mercenary?" he repeated, distorting the word a bit. "No. Being a mercenary has ugly connotations, like being a gun for hire. That isn't what we do at all. We're more like…" He thought for a moment, then went on. "Well, like a civilian rescue service. In many countries there is a huge gulf between the very rich and the rest of the population. There are all kinds of outlaws who think the rich are like fat, vulnerable piggy banks, and kidnapping is the way to open the vaults. It's practically a major industry in some countries. Family members are always being kidnapped and held for ransom." He gave her his quirky smile. "We specialize in getting them back."

"Really?"

He nodded. "Without paying the ransom, if possible."

"Oh."

"That's the major part of our mandate. We also do other things. We find lost cargo shipments. Get political refugees out of dangerous situations. Things like that."

"I see," she said, her gaze sliding over the open neck of his shirt, then turning back up to meet his eyes. "I didn't really understand that. I have to tell you, that makes me feel a little better about it."

He moved closer, taking in the scent of her hair. "About what kind of work I do?"

"Yes. I was sort of stuck on the outlaw element. Now I see that was wrong and that you could characterize it as humanitarian."

He touched her cheek, brushing off a crumb that had landed there. Her skin was luminous. She was so beautiful, it made his heart feel full of wonder. "You prefer to think of me as one of the good guys, huh?" he said huskily, leaning closer still.

"Of course."

She looked down but she didn't move away. He could see the pulse throbbing at the base of her throat. She wanted him to kiss her. There was no way he was going to be able to resist when it was so obvious she wanted his touch as much as he wanted hers.

"Darcy."

"Yes?"

She looked up. He dropped a soft kiss on her lips, light as a feather, then drew back.

"You'd better go," she whispered, her eyes dark as shadows.

He nodded. "I know," he said.

But he didn't go. He kissed her instead. He took her into his arms, sliding his body against hers. She sighed and when his mouth covered hers, her tongue was there to meet his. She felt hot and smooth and as the kiss deepened, she arched her body into his, pressing hard with her breasts, as though she needed to feel his strength against her most sensitive places. Rational thought slipped away and all he could think of was heat and moisture and his mouth on her nipples. When she cried out, at first he was sure she was giving him an invitation, but pretty quickly, even his libido-drugged mind understood she was trying to get him to stop.

They pulled apart, panting and still clinging, but no longer pressed so tightly together. Darcy was the first to manage a coherent sentence.

"Mitch, this is exactly why you shouldn't be here," she said breathlessly.

"I know." He kissed the tender area in front of her ear.

"Then what are you doing?" she cried, trying ineffectually to pull away.

He snuggled into the curve of her neck. "I think we should explore all the possibilities so we know what to guard against," he murmured.

She laughed softly, but that didn't change anything. Taking a deep breath, she forced him away.

"Look, we've already proven that you can seduce me at will," she said in a sort of mild despair. "It doesn't take much."

He touched her cheek, the side of his hand sliding gently down the length of her face while he smiled at her. "You know why that is, don't you?"

"No. Tell me."

He shrugged. "We're so damn compatible, you and me." He cupped her chin in his hand, studying her full, gorgeous lips. "That's why we ought to get married."

She closed her eyes and this time she managed to pull completely out of his reach. "Yeah. Right." She went into the hall and toward the sun porch, as though to lure him there and out of her hair. Looking back to see if he'd followed, she said firmly, "You know very well that I can't marry anyone who is not willing to be a father to my children."

He shook his head, frowning as he walked behind her. "What are you talking about? I'm a father. I know it happened while I wasn't paying attention, but you can't deny the biology of the situation."

She turned back to face him, looking sad in a way that made him crazy. "Biology isn't enough."

He reached for her but she dodged him. "Look, Darcy," he said. "I like them just fine. They're cute little kids."

She nodded. "You like them, but you don't love them."

He searched her gaze. "How do you know?"

"It's obvious. A vague sense of affection won't do it. I need a man who is prepared to go all the way." She flattened her hand over her chest. "I need a man who feels it right here. In the heart."

In the heart. He could do that. Couldn't he? Why not. "Darcy," he began, not sure what he was going to say but determined to defend himself.

"Good night, Mitch," she said, leaving him at the door to the porch. "Breakfast is at seven. See you then."

He watched her go. Everything about her appealed to his senses, but also to his mind and heart. She was the whole package as far as he was concerned. The only problem was, he wasn't in the market for what she offered. Could he change his life around in order to accept delivery? He couldn't make promises like that. Not yet. Maybe never.

The light, airy feeling of joy and buoyancy he'd felt with her was gone. Sadness and uncertainty was back. He wasn't sure this story was going to get its happy ending.

It was earlier than seven when Mitch woke up in his cot on the sunporch. He knew right away that he wasn't alone. He felt something move on one side, and then someone was sitting on his arm on the other. He looked up and found a pair of bright blue eyes staring right down at him. Looking to the right, he met another pair of eyes. It was the twins, both making odd gurgling noises. He blinked at them sleepily, not sure if he was pleased that they'd come for an early morning visit or annoyed that they had interrupted his sleep.

His first impulse was to call for Darcy to come and get these little monsters off him but he stopped himself. After all, these were his kids, too. He ought to get to know them a little better. So he managed a lopsided grin at the two of them. They were sure cute. He was going to have to learn which was which so he could call them by name.

But he began to notice something strange. He hadn't remembered them with such round faces before. Their cheeks seemed awfully chubby. Then he realized they were both chewing on something, and a stream of shiny blue drool began to drip down one small chin.

"Hey," he said. "What's in your mouth. What have you got in there?"

The drooler opened his mouth obediently, revealing a large mush of multicolored jell. His brother immediately did the same.

"Oh my God!"

Mitch craned his neck to look at his desk. Sure enough, his large jar of jelly beans was standing empty.

"Darcy!"

He jumped out of bed and grabbed one boy, trying to pry his jaws back open. The boy began to yell and Darcy burst into the room and cried, "What are you doing?"

He looked up, his hand full of a sickeningly sticky mass. "I'm trying to prevent a jelly bean poisoning incident," he told her crossly, holding out his hand and gazing at it in horror. "You'd better get the other one," he added, as twin number two toddled quickly from the room. "He's got a mouthful of them, too."

Darcy dashed after him, but he could hear her laughing. That reassured him a bit. He'd been afraid that this might have actually done real damage, but if Darcy was taking it lightly, maybe he could relax. He picked up his charge and carried him into the house until he found Darcy at the kitchen sink, rinsing out number two's mouth.

"Which one is he?" he asked.

She glanced up and took in his lack of attire, her eyes widening. Quickly she turned away. "Uh, you've got Sean. I've got Sammy," she said, doing an exchange and starting on the next boy. In a few minutes they were both cleaned up and had been set on their feet and had run for cover, both whimpering a bit. Losing those jelly beans seemed to be a major tragedy in their young eyes.

"They hate me now, don't they?" he said ruefully.

"No." She shook her head, bending to clean up the sink. Anything to keep from looking at that beautiful naked torso. "They don't hate you."

"But they don't understand. They probably just think I'm a mean old guy who won't let them touch his jelly beans."

She bit her lip and willed him to turn and walk away before she had to face him. But it seemed he wasn't going anywhere. Taking a deep breath, she was the one who turned. She gazed into his blue eyes and tried to keep from noticing anything else. But that was like ignoring the elephant in the room.

"You're not dressed," she said.

He looked down as though this was the first he'd known of it. "I've got on pajama bottoms," he said defensively.

That he did—lightweight, flimsy things, barely hanging onto the hard bones of his hips and slumping down precariously between them. It didn't take much imagination to see him as though he didn't have on anything at all. One glance down and she felt as faint as a nineteenth century Southern belle before she'd found her smelling salts.

"Listen," she said, suddenly breathless. "Go get dressed and come on back and we'll have breakfast."

He grinned. He knew she was in jitters over this. "Why don't I just come on into the kitchen and help you?" he teased.

She jabbed him in his chest with her forefinger. "You go get your clothes on," she ordered.

"Okay, I will," he said reluctantly, smiling into her eyes. "If you kiss me."

"What? No, it's too early in the morning."

He hovered close. "Kiss me and I promise I'll be good for…oh, at least an hour."

She couldn't resist an answering smile. "Three hours," she countered.

"An hour and a half."

"Deal."

His lips touched hers and she closed her eyes, savoring the sweetness of his token of affection. When she opened them, he was still there, looking down at her with a bemused smile on his face. She glanced at his chest, then reached out to touch the fiery scar.

"How did that happen?" she asked him.

"A knife fight in a bar," he said dismissively. "Nothing to worry about."

She frowned, searching his eyes. She didn't believe him. Someday she was going to get him to tell her the truth.

He kissed her again. She kissed him back. This time he drew away and left the room, but she couldn't open her eyes. She stood there for a long, long moment, letting the glow of him wash over her. And when she finally regained her sanity, she was smiling. What was that warm feeling inside? Ah yes, she remembered it now. It was something very close to happiness.

Mitch wasn't sure how he was going to like having breakfast with the twins, but in the end, he had a great time. The boys were little barbarians and Darcy definitely had her hands full with them. He was surprised to find that a word of warning in his deeper voice could stop them in their tracks where Darcy's pleadings went unheeded. But all in all they were good kids, if a bit rambunctious.

He enjoyed watching them, especially when Sean began laughing uproariously because Sammy had somehow figured out how to make milk shoot out of his nose. Darcy put her head in her hands in despair, but Mitch laughed right along with the boys. He looked from one to the other and couldn't stop grinning.

Something was clanging deep down in his memory file. This scene seemed so familiar. He couldn't pin down the specifics, but he was sure he and his brother had been there, done that. These were great little boys, really. Great little rowdy boys. How could he not like them? How could he not feel an affinity to them and their pranks?

"Hey guys," he said, gazing at them both. "What else have you got planned to drive your mother crazy with today?"

Sammy stuck his spoon to his nose and Sean began dropping bits of cereal over the side of his high chair tray, leaning over to watch as the kernels jumped and scattered. Mitch looked at Darcy and she looked at him and they both started to laugh in a helpless fashion. Funny, in all that mess and confusion, the thought came to him that life was good.

CHAPTER NINE

BY LATE in the morning, Darcy had developed enough confidence in Mitch's relationship with the boys to leave them with him while she went to the store. It should have been a quick trip. She just needed bread and enough milk to make up for the supply Sammy had wasted at breakfast with his nose-spewing antics. But it seemed like she ran into people she knew down every aisle and everyone wanted to hear how Mimi was and where she was and how her sister was doing. So it was a bit later than she'd expected when she got back and she hurried from the car, feeling anxious.

"Hello," she called, coming into the house with her arms full. "Where is everybody?"

No answer. Her heart began to beat just a little faster. She stowed the bags onto the kitchen counter and began a search. One room after another turned up empty and they weren't out back. The garage was cold and silent. By now she was beginning to feel a bit frantic. Mitch's car was still out front. Where could they be? She ran out into the street and looked up and down. What now? Should she call the police? She turned back toward the house, and at the same moment, she heard a dog bark.

"Sparky?"

She ran toward the sound, realizing it was coming from the path between the houses that led to the canyon. And there they were, coming back through the weeds, Mitch carrying a boy in each arm. Tears of relief popped into her eyes and she ran to meet them. Sparky barked and danced around them as she took Sean from Mitch.

"I'm glad you showed up," Mitch said, looking tired. "These guys are heavy."

"What were you thinking?" she demanded. "They're too young to go to the canyon."

"I guess you're right," he said ruefully. "They pooped out about half way there."

She shook her head. They barely knew how to walk and he had them hiking to the canyon? It was obvious he didn't know much about little boys this age. But then, how could he? At least he'd wanted to do something with them instead of planting them in front of the television or putting them in a playpen.

"Oh good, you put on their little tennis shoes," she noted as Sean snuggled close, his eyelids drooping. She saw the burrs in their socks and shook her head. He'd actually had them walking through the weeds. Suddenly she was chuckling.

"Oh, Mitch, you're a peach," she said, gazing at him with blatant affection.

"And you're the apple of my eye," he countered, pretending to look sultry. "So I guess that makes us even. Sort of."

"Sort of," she agreed, leading the way into the house.

They put the babies down for their naps and she went into the kitchen to put away the groceries. He followed her there.

"Oh, by the way. Your friend Kevin called while you were out."

"He did?" She looked up in surprise. "What did he want?"

"I don't know." Mitch grinned. "He was quite amazed when I answered the phone."

She grinned back. "I'll bet he was."

He smirked, raising one eyebrow significantly. "I don't think he'll be calling again."

"Mitch! What did you say to him?"

"Nothing. I just let him know he didn't have a chance with you now that I'm back in town."

"What?" She pretended to be outraged, but she really couldn't muster the emotion for it. After all, he was right. Now that Mitch was here, no other man had a chance of catching her attention. The only thing was, who knew how long he would stay?

Just after lunch, Darcy went out to the street to get the mail from Mimi's mailbox. She pulled out a magazine, some bills and a postcard from an old college friend, and as she was reading the note on the back, a long, low Cadillac pulled up alongside her. She turned and looked curiously as Mitch's mother leaned across the seat and sent the window down.

"Miss Connors, may I speak to you for a moment?" she asked.

Darcy was surprised, but she recovered quickly. "Of course. It's nice to see you, Mrs. Carver."

The woman motioned for her to get into the car and she did so, sliding into the passenger's seat and turning to face the older woman. Mrs. June Carver was expensively dressed and coiffured and it was quite evident she'd once been a very beautiful woman. Diamonds sparkled on her fingers, gold chains accented her dress.

"I understand my son is staying here with you," she said, turning off the engine and settling back to talk.

Darcy studied the woman, noting the tragedy shadowing her eyes. Her natural reserve melted. She felt nothing but compassion for Mrs. Carver at the moment, despite the coolness the woman had exhibited toward her in the past.

"Yes, he is."

June Carver sighed. "He's very angry with me. I know that. I want to get beyond that, though. And I'm hoping you'll help me."

Darcy shook her head. "I don't know how I can do that," she said. "He hasn't really talked about his disagreement with his family," she added quickly. "I don't know much about it."

Mrs. Carver drew a breath deeply into her lungs and began to explain. "I'm afraid I exaggerated his father's condition in order to lure him home under somewhat false pretenses. Once he found out the truth, he was furious."

Darcy shook her head. "I'm afraid I still don't understand."

The woman stared at her for a long moment as though trying to decide how much to tell her. Finally she went on.

"Both of my sons became estranged from their father years ago, and that meant that I hardly ever see either one of them. I wonder if you can understand the pain a mother feels in such a situation. I love my boys deeply. Having no contact was torture for me." Her hands tightened on the wheel. "I finally found Mitch and told him his father had suffered a heart attack and we needed him home to help keep the company from falling into the hands of certain rival factions who have always borne us ill will."

"Ned Varner," Darcy guessed softly.

Mrs. Carver nodded. "Yes, Ned has always tried to wrestle control of the company away from my husband. I knew Mitch's competitive spirit would respond to that appeal. He promised to come home for one year to make sure that the worst didn't happen."

Darcy shook her head, studying the woman. "Was it all a lie?"

"Not really." She sighed. "But it wasn't the whole truth, either. Robert does have a heart condition and he could have an attack at any time. And he was in the hospital, but for a minor angioplasty, not a full-fledged heart attack."

"So Mitch found that out."

"Yes."

Darcy frowned, thinking about things he'd said. "But he hasn't threatened to leave, has he?"

She hesitated. "No. Actually he seems to be tied up in some sort of competition for a contract that he doesn't want to lose." She half smiled. "As I said, his competitive spirit seems stronger than ever. So he may stay for that full year after all."

"But if you don't see him…"

"Exactly. I'm right back where I started. And that's where you come in."

"Me?"

"Yes. Please, Miss Connors…"

"Call me Darcy."

"Darcy, then. If you care for my son at all, I'm sure you would want him to have good relations with his family."

She looked pathetic and Darcy was sure it was very difficult for a woman with her pride to let herself come this close to being seen as a miserable beggar for the kindness of strangers.

"If you could convince him to come back and just talk to us…to his father…that would be wonderful."

Reaching out, she covered Darcy's hand with her own. "I'm not asking you to make a commitment. Just think it over and do what you think is best. But please understand how much we love him." Her eyes were brimming with tears. "And how much we want him back on speaking terms with us both."

On impulse, Darcy covered the woman's hand with her own. "Mrs. Carver, I happen to think that family relations are among the most precious possessions we are blessed with. And sometimes the hardest to maintain. I will do what I can. You can count on me. But whether anything I say will have any weight with your son is another story. I can't promise that."

Mrs. Carver closed her eyes for a moment and her tears slipped down her powdered cheeks. "Thank you. Darcy, you don't know how grateful I am."

Darcy smiled. "I'd better go in," she said. "If you'd like to see Mitch…"

She shook her head. "No. Not right now. But I do appreciate this, Darcy. I'll be in touch."

Darcy walked into the house slowly. Detouring past the French doors, she looked in at where Mitch was working. He looked up and smiled, and she waved, but she didn't go in. She had to think over what his mother had told her. She knew instinctively that his relationship with his parents was directly related to what his relationship with her and her boys would be. She wanted to do this right.

Darcy was getting the boys up from their nap when Mitch came looking for her.

"Here you are," he said, coming into the boys' room and grinning at their sleepy faces. "Listen, have you given any thought to how we should attack the Heartland Project?"

"No," she said a bit testily. Dealing with two toddlers at one time did tend to put her nerves on edge at times. "I'm a little busy right now."

"So I see. Here, I'll take Sammy."

She handed him over gratefully, then stopped and looked at the picture Mitch made with the little blond head on his shoulder. Her heart skipped a beat. Father and son—it was just too perfect.

Taking Sean out of his crib, she put him on the changing table and reached for the baby powder on the shelf above it. Unfortunately she jostled the shelf and the whole thing tipped, spilling the contents to the ground.

"Oh, this stupid shelf system," Darcy cried, leaning down to pick up the baby powder, along with two stuffed animals that had slid off the shelf as well. "We're going to have to try to find a local handyman to fix this thing before it comes down on top of us all."

Mitch gazed around at the room. "Actually there's quite a bit you could do here to fix this up," he mused.

"The boys should have a better room. Something decorated to their tastes and better equipped for their needs."

She glanced at him sideways. "I've got neither the time nor the money to do much renovating."

He nodded, thinking as he gazed about. "I could fix this shelf system."

She turned, astonished. "You?"

"Sure, me. Why not?"

A slow grin crept over her face. "I didn't know you were handy. In that around-the-house way, I mean."

"Sure. All you need is a couple of screws in the right places. A hammer. Some nails. Hey, I'll take care of it this afternoon."

Darcy shot him a quizzical look, but he hardly noticed. He was in a state of shock himself. After all, what was he saying? He knew about as much about using a power saw as he knew about using a lacrosse bat. He was pretty darn handy at making his way over guarded borders and hacking his way through jungles, but he'd never learned how to do normal household maintenance. It had only been in the last few weeks or so that he'd even lived in a normal house again. His father had never been one to bond over teaching his son manly activities—and he'd never had much reason or interest in learning how to do basic carpentry on his own. And now he was going to strap on a tool belt and come to the rescue? Was this really going to work?

Oh well. No real problem. After a couple of

seconds of apprehension, he settled down. He was pretty sure he could figure out how to use a hammer and a screwdriver. One thing he had learned in his precarious way of living was how to use the resources he found around him. He would probably do okay once he got into it.

"You know," Darcy was saying, "Kevin is an amateur carpenter. He does very nice woodworking. Maybe we should call him to come over and give us a hand."

That would be the day. He heard the slightly teasing tone in her voice and knew she was goading him. But he didn't take the bait. He was going to figure out how to do this on his own, just like the man of the house would do. He smiled to himself, feeling good about it. This was something he probably should have learned how to do years ago. Better late than never. He gave the little boy in his arms a hug, feeling the wonder of such vibrant life so near. He wanted to do something for these kids. After all, who knew how long he would be around to watch them grow?

He helped Darcy finish cleaning up the boys and put them into the playpen for a bit of playtime before a planned trip to the park. He was wondering where he was going to find the tools to do what he'd promised when Darcy gestured from the kitchen.

"Mitch, we need to talk," she said.

"Oh. Sure thing."

He followed her into the kitchen. She'd set out tall

glasses of iced tea and they both sat down at the kitchen table to sip on them. It wasn't until he took his seat that he noticed the look on her face and began to feel a quiver of apprehension.

"What's up, Darcy?" he asked.

Her gaze was clear and direct. "I saw your mother today."

He stiffened. "Where?"

"Out in front of the house. She was looking for you."

He digested that and nodded. "Why didn't she come in?"

"She wanted to talk to me. She asked me to give you a message."

"Great." His mouth twisted. "So she didn't have the nerve to meet me face-to-face? She has to send me messages now?" His anger was growing and he tried to leash it in. Getting angry usually meant you were going to do something stupid, and he didn't want that. "So what did she say?"

Darcy licked her lips. "She wants you to come by the house and speak to your father."

He snorted. "Cold day in hell," he muttered.

She winced. "I think you should go."

He looked at her as though he couldn't understand how she could say such a thing. "Darcy this has nothing to do with you."

"I know. But your mother…she looked so sad." Darcy shook her head wishing she knew the words that would persuade him. She had a feeling this was important, that he really should do this. But she knew "feelings" weren't going to change his mind.

"You don't know the background, Darcy. Our family is like those families they make movies about, where there are secrets tearing people apart. I know that sounds melodramatic, but in a way, it's true. There's a past here you don't understand. You can't fix things."

"That's probably true—that I don't understand. But Mitch…" She gazed at him earnestly. "Nothing is ever beyond repair. If you could see your mother. This is obviously tearing her apart. And maybe you *can* fix things if you just—"

"No." He rose from the chair, threw her an angry glance and turned on his heel. "Just stay out of this, Darcy. I won't go to see my father. Forget it."

Darcy sat and watched him stalk off. A warning her own mother used to make kept echoing in her head. *One thing you should always remember, Darcy. You watch how a boy treats his parents. That's the same way he'll treat you someday. Take a lesson from it.*

How he would treat *her* wasn't so important. How he treated the babies—that was the crux of the matter.

The rest of the week seemed to fly by. Their routine very quickly fell into patterns that fit both their lifestyles very well. Mitch spent most of the day working. Darcy spent most of the day with the children. The four of them came together for breakfast and lunch, but Darcy put the boys to bed before dinner, which she and Mitch had alone.

They had daily telephone calls from Mimi who was thinking she might be able to get home sooner than she'd thought when she left. Mitch and Darcy looked at each other when they heard the news. Neither of them said anything, but neither of them wanted this idyll to be over just yet. This time together seemed special, an oasis from the real world. And part of it, he had to admit, was being with the children. They would never be this age again. This little family would never be quite the same again, no matter what happened in their individual lives. This time was to enjoy.

Mitch worked on the shelf system in the boys' bedroom for two days before he began to get the hang of it, but now he was spending a lot of time at it, repairing things and building shelves everywhere he could find a need. He loved it and was proud of his work. Darcy was proud of it, too, but she was beginning to worry he was going to overrenovate if she didn't hold him back.

"We've got to do something with the walls in this bedroom," he said when he finished the shelving. "It needs something."

"A fresh coat of paint?" she suggested.

"More than that. It needs murals."

"Mitch, you're not an artist," she said quickly, alarmed.

"No. I'm not. But I know one."

"Who?"

"Ginger Hiro. I went to school with her. She works in Graphics at ACW nowadays. I'll bet she'd do it for us."

"That might be nice." Darcy mused, looking the area over. "I could see bunnies on the wall."

"Bunnies?" he said with scorn. "Are you kidding? It's gotta be monkeys."

She frowned. "I don't know. Bunnies are sweet. Monkeys might encourage bad behavior."

"Monkeys," he insisted. "No wimpy little bunnies for my boys."

He went on as though he hadn't noticed what he'd said and the way he'd said it. But she had, and she stared at him. She had to admit, there had been a sea change in the way he treated the children. He obviously liked them a lot and they adored him. It made her heart swell just to watch them together. Was it enough? She wasn't sure. And it was his relationship—or lack of it—with his parents that gave her the most trouble now.

That same afternoon he asked how she was coming on plans for the Heartland Project and she finally had to come clean. She hadn't done a thing to help him, because she'd decided she wasn't going to do anything to help promote his chances.

He was stunned when she told him. He couldn't understand her reasoning.

"Okay, Mitch," she said at last, knowing this could very well drive an immutable wedge between them. She didn't know how to avoid that. She had to be honest with him. There was no point in pretending things were okay when they weren't.

"Okay, here's the deal. I'll only help you on one condition—that you make a pledge that if you win the contract, you'll stay and guide it all the way. That you'll see it out, make a commitment to complete what you've started. If you can't do that, I don't think you deserve to get the contract and I won't help you."

He stared at her, his gaze clouded. "You're talking about making a promise to stay for years."

Her chin rose defiantly. "Yes, I guess I am."

He shook his head as though he couldn't believe what he was hearing. "Basically you want me to promise to put down permanent roots. To pledge not to leave for a very long time, no matter what."

She looked into his eyes and was chilled by the hard, cold look she saw there. He was not taking this well. But she couldn't let herself crumble.

"That's about it," she said firmly, though she was quivering inside.

His eyes narrowed. "You know I can't do that."

A wave of desolation swept over her. "Can't you?"

"No. Of course not. And I'm surprised that you would even suggest it."

She closed her eyes and turned away. "That's that, then."

He stared at her, anger simmering deep in his bones. He couldn't believe she was asking this of him. She knew better. She'd known from the beginning that he would have to go.

And so she thought she might be able to force him to do things her way by denying him the help he needed. That was what made him angry. He felt betrayed. He'd counted on her and now she'd turned on him. He would show her. He would win the damn contract without her help. He'd been depending too much on her as it was.

But he knew he was only blustering. As the first flush of his anger faded and he let it ebb and flow, he began to think it over a little more sanely. He knew she had her reasons, and that those reasons were valid by her lights. He also knew very well that her concern about the Heartland Project was nothing but a metaphor for her concern about him becoming a permanent part of the life of her family—someone who was around. And that she was losing hope.

That hurt. Didn't she know he was in love with her? That he'd loved her since that night in Paris? That he was crazy about the twins, too?

Yes, she knew. But she was letting *him* know that it wasn't enough. And maybe she was right. Maybe the pull of that other world he lived in was just too strong for him to ignore. He wasn't sure yet. He just didn't know.

That night he decided to tell her about his fight

with his father. Maybe that would help her to understand him a little more. He waited until the boys were asleep and their dinner was finished and the dishes washed. Darcy made them each a cup of hot cocoa and they sat side by side at the kitchen table while he explained how it had happened—the betrayal that had shaped his life.

"It was the summer after my freshman year in college. I was pretty full of myself. I came home to work at ACW for the summer and I brought my girlfriend with me. Kristi was from Baton Rouge. She was so pretty, with that sort of late teenage bloom. Not very bright, but the sort of girl a dumb kid of nineteen thinks is just terrific. I was pretty crazy about her. I got my father to give her a job in the typing pool. We had a great summer planned."

"Sounds like a pretty typical summer during the college years," Darcy said, trying not to feel a ridiculous flash of jealousy.

"Sure. But I was the boss's son, heir to the throne and all that. I thought I was hot stuff and I thought that Kristi thought so, too."

Darcy smiled at the picture he was painting, though she knew the way he was presenting it meant he was setting himself up for some sort of fall.

"I got assigned to go out to the Panhandle for a few days, to meet with some farmers, look at some land, make some evaluations. The whole time I was out there, I was thinking about getting back to Kristi. I got a chance to hitch a ride and got back early. I went straight into work, even though it was the lunch hour, and went to leave my paperwork on my father's desk." He shook his head ruefully. "Only Kristi had gotten there before me. She and my father were doing some extracurricular work right there in his office."

"Oh, Mitch." Darcy had known it would be bad but she hadn't quite expected this. It hit her like a sock in the stomach.

"I always had a suspicion that my father played around a bit. I hoped that my mother didn't know. I was always a bit too protective of her from the time I was a little boy. It always seemed like she was good and my father was not quite good enough." He shook his head again. "But to find him doing my girlfriend was a bit much. Like a fool, I raced home to get my mother to pack up her things and let me take her away from the cad she was married to." He laughed shortly. "She told me to mind my own business and pick a better girl next time." He winced, hurt by that even now. "I felt like my world had fallen off its axis."

She pulled her arms in tightly, wanting to give him a hug but not sure he wanted her to. "So you took off."

"Exactly. I did just what I knew they would hate the most—quit college, joined the Army and went to see the world. I didn't want to see either one of them ever again."

"I can understand that."

"Can you?" He looked up at her, his gaze intent.

"Can you really, Darcy? Can you understand how deep that break in trust was? How much it hurt? How I can't forgive, even today?"

The pain was plain in his eyes. Reaching out, she covered his hands with hers. "I'm so sorry," she murmured.

He seemed to shake himself. "Yeah, well, that was a long time ago. A lot of water under the bridge." He cleared his throat.

She nodded. "You know you've got to forgive him," she said softly, knowing he would reject that out of hand, but needing to say it.

"What?" He looked at her like she was crazy.

"Has your mother forgiven him?"

"I suppose so, but…"

"Then you can, too." Her fingers tightened around his hands. She stared into his eyes, trying hard to convey just how serious she was about this. "I'm not saying this for him. I'm saying it for you. Mitch, you're the one I care about."

He was shaking his head, but he was also searching her eyes, looking for answers in the dark depths of them. "Why do you care about me?" he asked her huskily.

She blinked and straightened slightly. "Why do you think? You're the father of my children."

He turned his hands so that they were holding hers. "And?"

"That's enough."

He started to smile. "Liar," he whispered. He pulled her closer. "Tell me the truth."

She half laughed, captured by him. "Which truth are you talking about?" she teased evasively, even as she turned her face up to him. She was just glad he wasn't angry with her. If they could keep from arguing, they might have a chance to find common ground.

"This one," he said, beginning to drop nipping kisses on her full lips. "Tell me how much you like me, Darcy Connors."

"I like you lots, Mitch Carver," she said earnestly, succumbing to his kisses without making any effort to fight them. "Lots and lots."

"Lots better than any other guy?"

She snuggled against him. "Lots better," she agreed with a happy sigh.

"Good." He buried his face in her hair, holding her close. "I like you lots and lots, too."

Darcy closed her eyes. It was heaven being here with him this way. But why couldn't either one of them mention the 'l' word out loud? Was admitting there was love between them going a step too far? Did it create a commitment neither one of them dared make? Were they scared? Or just too cautious?

Funny—they managed to get the silly playfulness of lovers down pat. But the spirituality completely eluded them.

CHAPTER TEN

THE next morning Mitch awoke to an attack from the twins. They were taking turns climbing up on his desk chair and jumping off onto his stomach as he lay on the cot, laughing maniacally all the while.

"Darcy!" he called pitifully. "Help!"

That made the twins laugh even harder and by the time Darcy came running in, they were lying on either side of him, convulsed in hiccups and he had a hard time convincing her of what they'd been doing.

"They never did that," she insisted. "Even if they could climb up on the chair, how did they manage to jump? They can't jump. They're babies."

"They're baby monsters," he grumbled sleepily, but not too sleepily to notice Darcy was still in her robe, and that the boys had jumped off the cot and were headed back into the house as fast as their chubby little legs could take them. "The spawn of their monster mom."

"Oh, and I suppose their monster dad had nothing

to do with it?" she countered, standing over where he lay, pretending to be stern.

"Come here, monster Mom," he muttered, grabbing her when she bent too close and pulling her down onto the cot with him. She came with a shriek and they wrestled for a moment, laughing. Mitch took the opportunity to pull her soft body close. Her unbound breasts felt so soft he almost groaned aloud when he touched them. She pulled away quickly, and just as she did, the front doorbell rang.

She looked at him. He was suddenly alert.

"Who could this be?" she wondered, tying her robe tightly and hurrying toward the front of the house.

Before Mitch had fully pulled on his own robe, she was back. "It's your mother," she said, her cheeks flushed.

June Carver was right behind her.

"Mitch," she said, going directly to him and taking his hands. "Your father has had a heart attack."

A tiny tremor of shock went through him, but he managed to hide it. "No kidding?" he said, his voice dripping with sarcasm. "I think I've heard that one before."

Mrs. Carver slapped her son, shocking him and stunning Darcy.

"Mitchell Carver, you have been acting like a snotty brat ever since you came back from overseas. It's time to grow up. Your father is not a perfect man. Neither are you. We all have our problems. Get over it."

She was shaking with emotion. Darcy could see that her state was affecting Mitch even more than her slap had.

"Your father has done many wonderful things for you in the past. You've blotted them all out in order to keep your anger churning against him. It's time you gave that up." Her eyes filled with tears and her voice shook. "Your father loves you. He thinks the world of you. It's been a horrible burden for him all these years to have a beloved son hate him so."

"That's pretty much his own fault," Mitch responded, ignoring the imprint of her hand on his face. Darcy noticed the sarcasm was gone and his look had lost its hardness.

"Yes. It is. And he knows that." She wavered, shaking her head, and her voice took on a more pleading tone. "He's a different person now, Mitch. He's in the hospital. He needs to see you. If you would only give him a chance…"

"I'm not a pushover like you are, Mom." He pulled the tie of his robe more tightly. "But I will come and see him. If it makes you happy."

Darcy closed her eyes and sighed with relief.

"Have you found Dylan?" Mitch said, speaking of his brother who was missing the same way Mitch had been.

"No. No, Mitch, it's just you and me to take care of your father." She lifted her head and stared at her son. "If you have the guts to do it."

Darcy left the room. The emotion between mother and son was too raw to include outsiders, and that was definitely what she was. She was sorry Mr. Carver was ill, but she was so glad Mitch was willing to make an effort to see him. If he could find a way to repair his family, maybe… Well, she didn't dare think things like that. Not yet.

Mitch went to see this father that morning, and in the afternoon, he went again, and Darcy went with him. They took the boys. Mitch had decided, with his father hovering near danger, it was time to introduce him to his grandchildren.

The twins were a hit. June Carver cried. Mr. Carver didn't cry, but he couldn't speak for quite a while. They both watched the babies and fell in love.

Darcy was overwhelmed with emotion. It was a joy to see these people admire the twins as much as she did. She laughed and encouraged the boys to show off and enjoyed the entire experience. But when she looked into Mitch's face, she saw shadows there. He wasn't completely won over to this new close family situation she was hoping to build. And that gave her chills.

That night they spent some time talking things over and she told him how glad she was he was opening to his family, even if just a crack.

"We all have things in our lives we're ashamed of," she reminded him. "Look at us. We shouldn't have done what we did in Paris. But we did it. It's over. And now we have these beautiful children."

"We redeemed ourselves," he said wryly. He grabbed her hand in his. "Only you did all the hard lifting," he acknowledged. "Darcy, have I told you lately how much I appreciate you?"

Appreciation was nice. Love would be better. She bit her lip and smiled a bit sadly.

The next day the medical news was good. Mitch's father was out of immediate danger. But Mitch came back from the hospital as full of anger as he'd ever been. Darcy didn't know what his parents had said or done to set him off, but he was fuming when he walked in the door.

"You see, Darcy, this is exactly why I have to get out of here," he said, pacing the floor. "They drive me crazy. I *am* getting out of here. I'm going back overseas where I belong."

He stopped and took her shoulders in his hands, looking down into her eyes with all the passion she wished could be channeled into love instead of anger. "But, Darcy, this time you and the boys are coming with me."

She stood very still, staring past him and out the window. It was a step. He was admitting how much he needed her and the babies. But she knew his scenario wasn't realistic. It just wasn't going to happen. It couldn't happen.

"What about the Heartland Project?" she asked him as he returned to pacing.

He hesitated, then shook his head. "The funny thing is I think I've got that one in the bag, if I want it," he told her, looking rueful.

She turned to look at him. "What makes you say that?"

"Ry Tanner got in touch with me the other day. I went out there this morning before I went to the hospital. He'll sell, but only to me."

Oh my. That was huge.

"But instead of taking advantage of that tremendous opportunity, you want to chuck it all and run overseas?" she asked, incredulous.

His gaze was rock hard. "You got it."

She shook her head, incredulous. Didn't he see how nuts this was?

"So you're going to throw out everything just so you can do it again—hurt your parents. Make them pay for not being who you wish they were. You'll wave the Heartland Project in front of them, show them what could have been, and smash it all to bits while you run off to play soldier games in foreign countries."

Darcy was angry. She was more angry than she'd ever been in her life. Finally she felt she was seeing things as they really were. And trying to make him see them, too.

He stopped and looked at her, his eyes narrowed. "You don't approve."

"That is putting it mildly. I think it stinks."

He ran a hand through his hair, looking tortured. "Why am I getting the sense that you have no intention of going with me?" he said softly.

"You got that right. You want me to pack up the boys and rip out our roots and follow you to God knows where, just so you can run again?" She shook her head firmly. "No. That's not going to happen."

He stood staring at her. "Darcy, listen," he began.

But she shook her head even more vehemently. "No, Mitch. You listen. You can't keep running away from your problems." She grabbed him by the lapels and forced him to look down at her. "I'm begging you, please don't do it. Stay here and learn to deal with things. Learn to forgive and to ask for forgiveness. Give the rest of the world a little slack. I'll stand by you forever if you do that." Letting go of his lapels, she took a step back, away from him. "But I won't run with you."

He stared at her for a long moment, then turned on his heel and left the house. She felt the tears coming and this time she let them fall. Was she really going to lose him again?

Mitch was preparing to leave. Mentally, emotionally, he was ready for it. He stopped by a packing shop to pick up a couple of cardboard boxes and headed for Mimi's house. It was time to get this show on the road.

He slipped into the house and went straight to the sunporch, ready to pack up his things and get out of there. He could hear Darcy vacuuming the boys' bedroom. He hesitated only a moment. No, it would be better to avoid seeing her again. He stepped down onto the sunporch and found his sleeping cot was filled with something he hadn't expected.

All tangled in the comforter were Sean and Sammy and Sparky, and all three were sound asleep. He stood looking down at them, a lump in his throat. Something about the faces of these beautiful, innocent children struck directly into his soul. He slowly sank into a chair that sat beside the cot. Watching the babies, his heart filled with such raw, deep emotion, he choked. Funny, just a couple of weeks before, he hadn't even known Sean and Sammy existed. Now they were very near to being the most important people in his life. Could he really go off and leave them behind, not see those rascally smiles, those bright blue eyes filled with mischief, not watch them grow and change and become boys?

Had two boys ever been so loveable, so endearing? How could he turn his back on these beautiful children? How could he shut his family out of his life? Was he crazy?

He thought of the work he did overseas as humanitarian. Here he was planning to go off and do that sort of thing again. He'd spent the last decade of his life working around the world for anonymous people thinking he was doing good. It suddenly came clear to him that he just might want to rethink a thing or two about that. Why wasn't he focused on doing good for his own children? What about a woman that he cared about? What about his own family, the people he loved? Maybe it was time to clean up some messes and take care of his own.

He stared down at the boys and such love welled up in his heart, he could hardly breathe. Maybe this was what was really important right now.

"They've been waiting for you," Darcy said from the doorway where she'd been watching for a few minutes. "I guess they fell asleep."

He looked up at her and she could see the trouble in his eyes. She looked at the packing boxes strewn on the floor. If she let him leave again without saying a word, how could she face their children? She wasn't very good at begging but this was something she had to do. She couldn't let him walk out without one last try to change his mind.

"Mitch," she said, trying hard to keep the quaver out of her voice as she walked to where he was sitting and dropped to the floor in front of him. "Please don't go. Don't leave us." Resting her elbows on his legs, she looked up into his face and added softly, "I love you so much."

Her eyes were shining like stars. He took her face in his hands and looked down at her and even with tears filling her eyes, she could see the affection there.

"I love you, too, Darcy," he said huskily. "And I love Sean and Sammy." He smiled. "And I'm just beginning to realize there is no way I can leave you. You're a part of me, all three of you. There's nothing I can do about that. It just is."

Her smile radiated joy. "Oh, Mitch!"

"I belong with you, Darcy. And we all belong in Texas."

"Oh, Mitch, I'm so glad you see that. ACW will be glad, too. And everyone involved in the Heartland Project."

"It's going to be a fight," he warned her.

She nodded. "I'll be at your side, fighting next to you all the way," she promised.

"Great."

He drew her up and into his lap and kissed her, hard.

"Okay, we really need to get this done." He touched her chin and frowned. "Will you marry me?"

He asked as though it was a hard question, as though he had no idea what her answer might be. And that was only fair. She had been turning him down all month, after all.

She began to laugh. Will you marry me? he'd asked. She threw her arms around him.

"With bells on," she cried, suddenly exuberant.

He bent to kiss her again. The boys were stirring and that meant he had to get any lovemaking in fast.

Once the twins were awake, the action would really begin around here.

That made him laugh, deep in his throat. He'd just signed on for a very bumpy ride, but one that was going to be full of thrills as well as spills. And he'd be with Darcy, all the way.

And that was just how it ought to be.

* * * * *

SPECIAL EDITION

Life, Love and Family

These contemporary romances will strike a chord with you as heroines juggle life and relationships on their way to true love.

New York Times *bestselling author*
Linda Lael Miller
brings you a BRAND-NEW contemporary story featuring her fan-favorite McKettrick family.

Meg McKettrick is surprised to be reunited with her high school flame, Brad O'Ballivan. After enjoying a career as a country-and-western singer, Brad aches for a home and family…and seeing Meg again makes him realize he still loves her. But their pride manages to interfere with love…until an unexpected matchmaker gets involved.

Turn the page for a sneak preview of THE McKETTRICK WAY by Linda Lael Miller On sale November 20, wherever books are sold.

Brad shoved the truck into gear and drove to the bottom of the hill, where the road forked. Turn left, and he'd be home in five minutes. Turn right, and he was headed for Indian Rock.

He had no damn business going to Indian Rock.

He had nothing to say to Meg McKettrick, and if he never set eyes on the woman again, it would be two weeks too soon.

He turned right.

He couldn't have said why.

He just drove straight to the Dixie Dog Drive-In.

Back in the day, he and Meg used to meet at the Dixie Dog, by tacit agreement, when either of them had been away. It had been some kind of universe thing, purely intuitive.

Passing familiar landmarks, Brad told himself he ought to turn around. The old days were gone. Things had ended badly between him and Meg anyhow, and she wasn't going to be at the Dixie Dog.

He kept driving.

He rounded a bend, and there was the Dixie Dog. Its big neon sign, a giant hot dog, was all lit up and going through its corny sequence—first it was covered in red squiggles of light, meant to suggest ketchup, and then yellow, for mustard.

Brad pulled into one of the slots next to a speaker, rolled down the truck window and ordered.

A girl roller-skated out with the order about five minutes later.

When she wheeled up to the driver's window, smiling, her eyes went wide with recognition, and she dropped the tray with a clatter.

Silently Brad swore. Damn if he hadn't forgotten he was a famous country singer.

The girl, a skinny thing wearing too much eye makeup, immediately started to cry. "I'm sorry!" she sobbed, squatting to gather up the mess.

"It's okay," Brad answered quietly, leaning to look down at her, catching a glimpse of her plastic name tag. "It's okay, Mandy. No harm done."

"I'll get you another dog and a shake right away, Mr. O'Ballivan!"

"Mandy?"

She stared up at him pitifully, sniffling. Thanks to the copious tears, most of the goop on her eyes had slid south. "Yes?"

"When you go back inside, could you not mention seeing me?"

"But you're Brad O'Ballivan!"

"Yeah," he answered, suppressing a sigh. "I know."

She rolled a little closer. "You wouldn't happen to have a picture you could autograph for me, would you?"

"Not with me," Brad answered.

"You could sign this napkin, though," Mandy said. "It's only got a little chocolate on the corner."

Brad took the paper napkin and her order pen, and scrawled his name. Handed both items back through the window.

She turned and whizzed back toward the side entrance to the Dixie Dog.

Brad waited, marveling that he hadn't considered incidents like this one before he'd decided to come back home. In retrospect, it seemed shortsighted, to say the least, but the truth was, he'd expected to be— Brad O'Ballivan.

Presently Mandy skated back out again, and this time she managed to hold on to the tray.

"I didn't tell a soul!" she whispered. "But Heather and Darlene *both* asked me why my mascara was all smeared." Efficiently she hooked the tray onto the bottom edge of the window.

Brad extended payment, but Mandy shook her head.

"The boss said it's on the house, since I dumped your first order on the ground."

He smiled. "Okay, then. Thanks."

Mandy retreated, and Brad was just reaching for the food when a bright red Blazer whipped into the space beside his. The driver's door sprang open, crashing into the metal speaker, and somebody got out in a hurry.

Something quickened inside Brad.

And in the next moment Meg McKettrick was standing practically on his running board, her blue eyes blazing.

Brad grinned. "I guess you're not over me after all," he said.

✓ *Silhouette*®

SPECIAL EDITION™

brings you a heartwarming
new McKettrick's story from

NEW YORK TIMES BESTSELLING AUTHOR

LINDA LAEL MILLER

THE
McKETTRICK
Way

Meg McKettrick is surprised to be reunited
with her high school flame, Brad O'Ballivan,
who has returned home to his family's
neighboring ranch. After seeing Meg again,
Brad realizes he still loves her. But the pride
of both manage to interfere with love...until
an unexpected matchmaker gets involved.

—— McKettrick Women ——

Available December wherever you buy books.

I ♥

HARLEQUIN *Presents*

BROUGHT TO YOU BY FANS OF
HARLEQUIN PRESENTS.

We are its editors and authors
and biggest fans—and we'd
love to hear from YOU!

Subscribe today to our online blog at
www.iheartpresents.com

Get ready to meet

THREE WISE WOMEN

with stories by

DONNA BIRDSELL,
LISA CHILDS

and

SUSAN CROSBY.

Don't miss these three unforgettable stories
about modern-day women and the love
and new lives they find on Christmas.

Look for *Three Wise Women*
Available December wherever you buy books.

REQUEST YOUR FREE BOOKS!
2 FREE NOVELS PLUS 2
FREE GIFTS!

HARLEQUIN ROMANCE®

From the Heart, For the Heart

YES! Please send me 2 FREE Harlequin Romance® novels and my 2 FREE gifts. After receiving them, if I don't wish to receive any more books, I can return the shipping statement marked "cancel." If I don't cancel, I will receive 4 brand-new novels every month and be billed just $3.57 per book in the U.S., or $4.05 per book in Canada, plus 25¢ shipping and handling per book and applicable taxes, if any*. That's a savings of over 15% off the cover price! I understand that accepting the 2 free books and gifts places me under no obligation to buy anything. I can always return a shipment and cancel at any time. Even if I never buy another book from Harlequin, the two free books and gifts are mine to keep forever.

114 HDN EEV7 314 HDN EEWK

Name	(PLEASE PRINT)

Address	Apt.

City	State/Prov.	Zip/Postal Code

Signature (if under 18, a parent or guardian must sign)

Mail to the **Harlequin Reader Service®**:
IN U.S.A.: P.O. Box 1867, Buffalo, NY 14240-1867
IN CANADA: P.O. Box 609, Fort Erie, Ontario L2A 5X3

Not valid to current Harlequin Romance subscribers.

Want to try two free books from another line?
Call 1-800-873-8635 or visit www.morefreebooks.com.

* Terms and prices subject to change without notice. NY residents add applicable sales tax. Canadian residents will be charged applicable provincial taxes and GST. This offer is limited to one order per household. All orders subject to approval. Credit or debit balances in a customer's account(s) may be offset by any other outstanding balance owed by or to the customer. Please allow 4 to 6 weeks for delivery.

Your Privacy: Harlequin is committed to protecting your privacy. Our Privacy Policy is available online at www.eHarlequin.com or upon request from the Reader Service. From time to time we make our lists of customers available to reputable firms who may have a product or service of interest to you. If you would prefer we not share your name and address, please check here. ☐

HR07

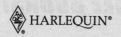

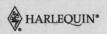

EVERLASTING LOVE™

Every great love has a story to tell™

Martin Collins was the man
Keti Whitechapen had always loved but
just couldn't marry. But one Christmas Eve
Keti finds a dog she names Marley.
That night she has a dream about
Christmas past. And Christmas present—
and future. A future that could include the
man she's continued to love.

Look for

by

Margot Early

Available December wherever you buy books.

HARLEQUIN Romance

Coming Next Month

In a month filled with Christmas sparkle, we bring you tycoons and bosses, loves lost and found, little miracles that change your life and always, always a happy ending!

#3991 SNOWBOUND WITH MR. RIGHT Judy Christenberry
Mistletoe & Marriage

Sally loves Christmastime in the small town of Bailey, with the snow softly falling and all the twinkling lights on the trees. But when handsome stranger and city slicker Hunter arrives, everything seems different, and she is in danger of losing her heart.

#3992 THE MILLIONAIRE TYCOON'S ENGLISH ROSE Lucy Gordon
The Rinucci Brothers

Ever heard the expression, to love someone is to set them free? Freedom is precious to Celia, since she can't see. But she can live life to the full! The last of the Rinucci brothers, Francesco, wants to wrap her in cotton wool, but hadn't bargained on feisty Celia....

#3993 THE BOSS'S LITTLE MIRACLE Barbara McMahon

Career girl Anna doesn't have time for love. She's poised for promotion, when in walks her new CEO, Tanner...the man who broke her heart a few weeks ago! Then Anna discovers a little miracle has happened—and it changes everything.

#3994 THEIR GREEK ISLAND REUNION Carol Grace

Even the most perfect relationships have cracks—as Olivia and Jack have realized. Their marriage seems over, but Jack refuses to let go. He whisks Olivia away to an idyllic Greek island. But will it be enough to give them a forever-future together?

#3995 WIN, LOSE...OR WED! Melissa McClone

Love it or loathe it, reality TV is here to stay! Millie loathes it, after irresistible bachelor Jace dumped her in front of millions of viewers. But in aid of charity, she finds herself on a new show with Jace, and *everything* is captured on camera—even their stolen kisses!

#3996 HIS CHRISTMAS ANGEL Michelle Douglas

Do you remember *that* guy? The one from your past that you loved more than life itself, the one you never seem to be able to get over? Imagine he's back in town, and more gorgeous than ever. Join Cassie as boy-next-door Sol comes home for Christmas....

HRCNM1107